THE SKY TOOK US

THE SKY TOOK US

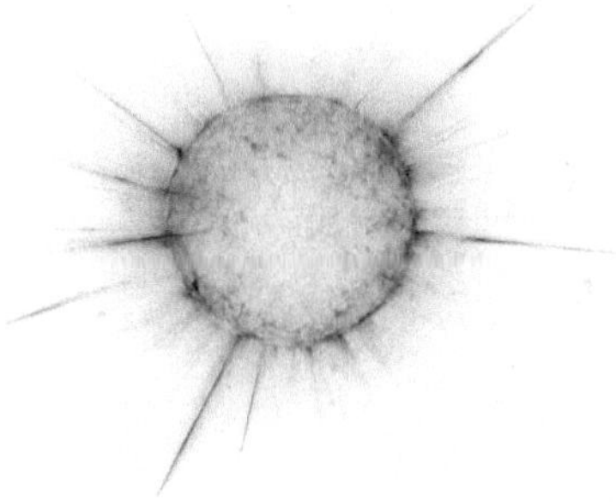

ANTHONY BONATO

AUBLIS PRESS

Aublis Press

Published by Aublis Press.

ISBN (*Paperback*): 978-1-0674262-0-0
ISBN (*E-book*): 978-1-0674262-1-7

Cover design by J Caleb Design. Book formatted for print and ebook by Phillip Gessert.

*"For small creatures such as we,
the vastness is bearable only through love."*

—CARL SAGAN

TABLE OF CONTENTS

CHAPTER 1

THE MOST DANGEROUS PROOF

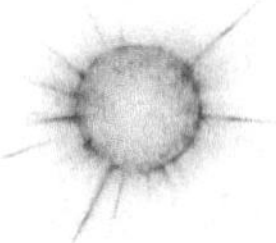

THE LOGIC HELD. Kris looked up from her calculations and steadied herself against the wall. No matter how she tested it, line by line, the conclusion stayed the same. For the first time all night, she allowed herself to think it. The proof might actually work.

Stacks of paper lay all over her bedroom, each filled with dense equations and intricate geometric figures. She tiptoed through the stacks, careful not to disturb them. The large whiteboard next to her desk reflected her work. Many of the equations written there felt like close friends; a few were long-lost acquaintances she'd been reunited with. Others were bitter enemies she'd made peace with after much struggle. She was afraid to believe it.

She'd always believed the Riemann hypothesis was too big for her. Too big for anyone. The conjecture about the zeros of the zeta function had eluded mathematicians for 170 years. To prove it, she needed to show that the solution to one particular equation had a certain form. A certain structure.

This one equation had defeated some of the greatest minds in mathematics. Many had tried their hand at proving it. Every one of them failed. But she had succeeded. Or at least she was 99 percent certain she'd succeeded. Maybe 98.6 percent.

She worked for three days straight, running on adrenaline. While her older sister, Antoinette, had been partying with her friends, Kris had been here, alone on the weekend as usual, with her papers, a whiteboard, the numbers, and eventually, a major breakthrough.

She drifted to the adjoining bathroom, with its dated green tiles and ten-year-old issues of *Scientific American*. Kris made a mess of the vanity as she splashed cold water on her face. A sixteen-year-old wasn't supposed to have dark circles under her eyes unless she put them there with eye shadow.

The idea hadn't arrived with fireworks. The pieces fit, locking into place. When the proof came together, she heard *the music*.

How to describe it? The music came from nowhere and everywhere. Serene. Otherworldly. Beautiful and cold, like a snowy Toronto day in January. She'd never told anyone about the music, worried they would think she was delusional. This time, the music had grown so loud it was deafening.

Kris had said nothing about her progress to her mom, who worried when her daughter retreated from the world. The roses blooming in the July sun had failed to lure Kris away from her work for days. She slept only a few hours and snuck out late to grab a sandwich. She mostly sipped black coffee and nibbled dark chocolate, the drug of choice for mathematical truth seekers—that chalky, 85 percent cocoa kind that turned her tongue brown.

An invisible force field had surrounded her, repelling every text and email. She hoped Mom and Antoinette would understand what she'd accomplished. They were all she had.

No one in the mathematical community would believe a teenager had proven the Riemann hypothesis, even a prodigy like Kris, who had completed her PhD months ago. Nate had fought endless battles with university committees to make it happen, arguing that genius didn't wait for birthdays. The media frenzy that had followed still unsettled Kris.

There was at least one person who would understand her proof, Kris thought. Even in 2035, only a small handful of people could understand this kind of mathematics. She was ready now, confident enough, to share it with him. And although it was late on a Sunday night, there was a chance she could still reach him.

Nate's face popped up on her screen. He was handsome, with wavy brown hair and sharp brown eyes that shone with confidence, but he was too intimidating to have a crush on. Besides, Nate was an ancient thirtysomething, and she could never think of him that way. He was her tough doctoral supervisor who didn't take crap. Her hands trembled as he looked at her.

"Nate, I've got something to tell you. The proof is ready for you to see."

Kris woke up the next morning at her usual slow pace, rolling out of bed like a lazy crocodile and stumbling to the kitchen.

Monday, July 16, 2035. Ten a.m. My head hurts. Hungover from another late-night math party. Ugh. Whatever this was, it wasn't the kind adults complained about in movies. She closed the diary. Kris loved writing longhand, scratching out her words and symbols in black ink. It was so much more real than typing on a screen.

She sipped black coffee and rubbed her eyes. Sarah, her mom, had left a note on the screen of the fridge saying that she was running errands downtown. Kris drained her mug and shuffled to her sister's room. The poster of Joan Jett glared fiercely at her, black-eyed and raw, as she knocked on the door. There was no answer from Antoinette, so Kris went inside. The place was a mess, with clothes on the floor and dirty dishes on the dresser. Her sister's prized guitar lay on her bed. Kris wrote on an old-fashioned sticky note and stuck it to the guitar. She walked with care, making sure not to disturb any of the room's contents for fear of her sister's retribution.

She pulled her hair back into a ponytail, reminding herself to ask Antoinette to cut it so it would stop getting in her eyes. A screen popped up on the kitchen table, displaying her login page and her puppy dog avatar. Moving her finger across the screen, she scanned through her favorite links on Rix. The kitchen window's smart glass shifted its tint a shade darker, like it knew how morning light annoyed her.

An ad for lipstick popped up. The ad algorithms were way off. Antoinette was more the target audience for lipstick, being a traditionally "cool" eighteen-year-old. Kris liked to keep it simple. Her longish hair was her one extravagance. Antoinette was the one who wore makeup and got tattoos. Sarah had freaked out when she'd come home with an intricate geometric pattern tattooed on her shoulder. Kris had designed it for her, and that act of rebellion had gotten her sister grounded for a week. Antoinette also had boyfriends and played guitar—she said those things made her awesome. Kris wasn't sure she agreed.

"Good morning, baby," her mom said as her face popped up on the screen. Sarah was holding her phone so close that Kris could see the sweat forming on her temples.

"Hi, Mom. I've been alive for one hundred and forty-two thousand, four hundred and forty-four hours," Kris said. "Which I feel like officially makes me a very old baby."

Sarah's brown eyes and hair contrasted with Kris's green eyes and blond hair, which must have come from her father's side. Antoinette had once told her that her eyes were spooky, shining with an inner fire. Ant could be dramatic.

Today looked to be a boring day, but Kris still felt a tinge of excitement. She had made a decision—she was going to tell her family the news about the proof, even though Nate and his team of postdocs would have to work for weeks, possibly months, to verify it.

A headline popped up on one of her breaking news apps: ORB IN SANKOFA SQUARE.

"That's weird. Something's going on in the square," she said to her mom. Kris poured herself a much-needed second cup of coffee.

"I know. I'm there. I came over from the Eaton Centre. There's a crowd, even bigger than normal."

Sarah zoomed her phone out. Kris saw a mass of people behind her but didn't see anything unusual. The light from the clear sky over the square was brilliant, and even through the screen, it made Kris squint.

"It's on every news site. Open a screen and you'll see," Sarah said.

Kris swiped her finger over the screen projected on the kitchen table and asked for a second screen, which opened on the wall next to the fridge. It showed a perfect sphere sitting in the middle of the square, surrounded by people. White lights lit up its surface. Kris rubbed her eyes and moved closer to the screen. She paused the video and zoomed in on the sphere. The reporters were also calling it an orb.

"Sounds odd. Why not give it its proper name and call it a sphere?" asked Kris.

"It's floating there, flashing stuff. No one knows what it is. Maybe a new movie promo? Sorry," Sarah said to a stranger who'd just bumped into her. *She's such a good apologetic Canadian. She'd even apologized for apologizing too much*, Kris thought.

Kris fiddled with the second screen so that Sarah could see it too. "Do you see those patterns?" she asked.

"Yup. Listen, I have to finish my shopping here and then do my essay. I'll be late again tonight—my literature class is this evening." Sarah was working on her English degree part-time so she could be a teacher. Taking care of two girls alone used to be a full-time job when Kris was little. But now Sarah relied on the two of them to help with the daily chores. Being a math genius had its benefits; Nate made sure Kris got a postdoctoral stipend from the university to help with the family's expenses.

Even with that additional support, they lived in a cramped bungalow. To make ends meet, Sarah cleaned other people's houses three days a week, and Antoinette worked part-time as a cashier at Walmart. They didn't take family vacations or wear designer clothes.

Dots were appearing on the sphere now, repeating at regular intervals. Kris ran a stopwatch on the screen. The intervals were: three, five, seven, eleven, thirteen—prime numbers.

"Wait. Mom, see that?" After putting the screen on pause, she studied the patterns close up, her nose close to touching the screen, her breath clouding the shiny table. Then she leapt up. "I know what that is! It's the Petersen graph and graph minors. They call them snarks, or bridgeless cubic graphs with chromatic index four. I proved that thing about them last year. Remember?"

"I can't remember what you proved last week, baby," Sarah said. Her mom's voice was faint. Sarah usually made her feel centered, but not now.

"This is too strange," Kris said, and gripped her mug—a gift from Antoinette after her doctoral defense. That was one of the only times the three of them had celebrated as a family. It wasn't every day that a sixteen-year-old got a PhD, after all.

Sarah scowled at the mug through the screen. "I wish you wouldn't use that mug." It was white with red letters that spelled out the vulgar equation: $f(u)=c^k$.

"It's a pun. You don't say the word, you say 'f of u equals c raised to the power k.'"

"You still say something like the word. Make sure to eat something. I want to get back to my shopping before the crowd gets any thicker. Love you."

"I love you too."

Sarah's screen closed, and Kris opened three news screens. All of them showed the orb. After the patterns on the sphere had repeated for a minute or so, new, more complicated patterns emerged. Something was off about the sphere, the scene, the whole event.

To Kris, it was a *structured* pattern, despite the chaos. She couldn't make sense of the jumbled images without pausing the video. Most of them looked like random visual noise, but there were clues there that drew her deeper in.

"A math orb? Maybe it's a way to get kids interested in math," Kris mumbled.

The door opened and Antoinette walked in, her cheeks flushed from the heat outside, her shoulder-length black hair stuck to her damp neck. It was a scorcher outside for sure. She pulled her sunglasses down the bridge of her nose, crossed her arms, and stared at Kris.

"Did you touch my stuff?"

"No way."

"Swear it on Erdős?"

"Okay. On Erdős. I didn't."

Kris loved her older sister and had come to terms with Antoinette being jealous of the attention she got because of her mathematical talents. Kris was the undeniable prodigy of the family. When she and Antoinette fought, her sister often reminded Sarah how spoiled Kris was, citing occasions when she'd let Kris skip chores, like taking out the garbage or folding the laundry.

Antoinette had her own interests. She loved music and played guitar in a band, The Nettes, made up of longtime friends. This was the beginning of her gap year after high school. Sarah insisted she do a business degree, but Antoinette was planning to go to an arts school.

The years of homeschooling and research with Nate had shrunk Kris's social circle down to her immediate family. Her undergrad degree had taken her two years. She'd begun her doctorate at thirteen and finished it this past April, a few weeks after her sixteenth birthday. All she could remember doing her whole life was studying and mathematics. She wondered if she was more than her theorems or if the world saw only the degree and not the person beneath it.

People call me a genius, but what do they know? Kris thought. Her life didn't feel glamorous; she barely slept, and her days blurred together until she barely remembered living them. Her life consisted of math on a page and three letters pinned after her name.

"So, K, you've heard about that orb?" Antoinette said.

"Guess I'm not the only one interested in it."

"Sarah texted." Antoinette's latest thing was to call Sarah by her first name instead of Mom or Mother. "She's at Sankofa Square picking out her latest mom jeans."

With that, Antoinette retreated to her room and closed the door. Joan Jett glared at Kris again; at any moment, the rock star might jump out of the poster and launch into a roaring guitar solo.

Kris returned her attention to the video of the sphere, watching the patterns with laser focus. There was something familiar about them—she could feel it—but it was out of reach. To keep track of the patterns, she reached for her diary, filled with her daily musings and pages of dense mathematical notes.

The live video showed photographers shooting the orb, their flashes dancing with the white patterns on its surface. It was as if the orb were a celebrity caught unawares in the middle of the city, surrounded by paparazzi, a throng of fans looking on.

A reporter moved close to a group of police keeping people away from the orb. "We're here at Sankofa Square, where a black orb has appeared, floating above the ground, lights in geometric patterns beaming from its surface. No one seems to know where the orb, measuring about one and a half meters wide, is from or how it is suspended. Police are restricting access to the area, holding back a large and growing crowd of curious onlookers."

Kris shuddered as she watched the sphere. Her throat tightened. The thing didn't look right. It was out of place, like a lucid dream crumbling apart before she woke.

Antoinette burst into the hall, wide-eyed, a sticky note attached to her index finger. "Holy shit, you proved the Riemann hypothesis?"

◎ ◦ ◎

Kris stared groggily at her half-eaten peanut butter sandwich and placed the plate on the dusty glass table beside her. She curled up on the couch with a pad of paper covered with math. It was minutes after eleven a.m. now, and all her Rix screens showed the orb and its sparkling dance of lights.

"What is it?" Kris asked her phone.

"The orb? I've never encountered anything quite like it. It may be a movie prop or an optical illusion. Do you want me to look up similar optical illusions that match the orb?" the device responded in its singsong voice.

"No, that's okay," Kris said.

Antoinette laughed so loud that Kris could hear her through the walls. She was on the phone with her bandmate and best friend, Paula. The Nettes were practicing tonight in Paula's parents' basement. That meant Antoinette would be in a good mood today.

"When I play, it's like I lose myself," Antoinette always said. Kris felt that way about math. During long hours of working on math, she heard the music. It was so magnificent it made her want to float away.

Kris grabbed a brown pillow and clutched it like a teddy bear. She studied the patterns of peaks and valleys on the popcorn ceiling. Her eyelids were heavy, and she let go and fell asleep.

There was a faint whirring sound. Kris lay on the cool grass in her backyard, looking up at a night sky full of twinkling stars. She could make out Orion's belt and the Pleiades star cluster. That was odd, as the light pollution from the city usually obscured most of the stars. She lifted her hand, wet with moisture from the grass, toward the expanse.

The sound grew louder and louder—her whole body vibrated with it. Where was Antoinette? Where was Mom?

There was a distant voice coming from everywhere and from nowhere. It wasn't a male or female voice. It spoke a single word.

"Maker."

Kris woke with a start as Antoinette dropped her phone on the floor next to the sofa.

"Damn it. I keep dropping this thing like it's a basketball and I expect it to bounce back. Were you sleeping? Right, you were up all night proving your earth-shattering hypothesis."

Kris sat up on the sofa. A screen on the wall opposite them displayed the orb, covered in lights and patterns, as well as the people watching it. The crowd was thickening now, layers and layers of people. The patterns on the orb repeated again and again.

"Was I asleep long?" Kris asked, then covered her mouth as she yawned.

"Nope, maybe ten, fifteen minutes," Antoinette said.

"I had a weird dream. Did Mom call?"

"Nope. And everyone is going downtown to see the orb. Paula is there already. I'm going down there later."

"I'll come too and get an extra-large latte from The Uncommon," Kris said. She hated living in the burbs on days when she worked on math late, in no small part because of the coffee. Making your own didn't always cut it, and the closest place where Kris could replenish her caffeine levels was a Tim Hortons that was a long twenty-minute walk away.

"How sure are you about your proof?" She looked at Kris. "Because if you're right, things get even less normal."

"Oof. That's kinda scary. The proof works, but it's so long there could be something wrong hiding in it. I didn't want to tell you or Mom until I was more sure. I am now. Nate has it. He's checking it with his postdocs."

Antoinette's jaw tightened. "I guess that's what Nate's there for. Mom will be stoked. You'll have to buy her a new house with your million bucks for solving a Millennium Prize Problem."

Antoinette knew her stuff. Only Grigori Perelman in 2003 had solved one of the seven Millennium Prize Problems, considered the most difficult in all of mathematics. The rest were wide open. And the Riemann hypothesis was the prize among the prizes, believed by many to be the most difficult one of them all.

"Do you think Mom will let me get a dog?" Kris asked.

Antoinette shook her head. "Anyway, this is all terrific news, K, but you won't become a world-famous superstar until that orb thing goes away. It's on every channel. No one knows what it is or where it came from."

Kris winced at the gnawing in the pit of her stomach.

"I've got a terrible feeling about all this," she said.

CHAPTER 2

VANISHING ACT

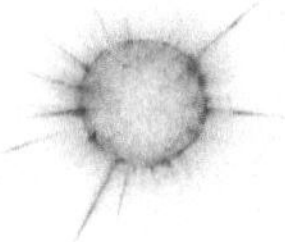

"THE CROWDS ARE huge now," Sarah said, her face projected on the wall of the living room next to the television. She stood several hundred meters from the seething crowd and still had to shout over the din. For about ninety minutes now, the orb had been flashing patterns on its black surface.

"Let's go to the square. Paula, Ryan, and Carolyn are there. Those freakazoids keep texting me about this gross older dude standing next to them who has bad BO and is smoking weed," Antoinette said.

Shouts from the news feeds interrupted them. The orb had quieted. The flashes had stopped.

"Is that it?" Antoinette asked.

"Mom, you should get out of there. Or at least move back. I don't like that orb or the mob," Kris said.

"It's perfectly fine. A few people got rowdy when someone threw a rock at the orb, but the cops have the crowds under control now. See?" Sarah panned the phone away from her face and toward the center of the square.

Kris swallowed hard; her hands were fidgety.

"You okay?" Antoinette asked.

"I...I feel horrible," Kris said, trembling. Her temples

throbbed. It wasn't from her math hangover. It was something else.

Antoinette shrugged.

"I did all my shopping," Sarah said, bringing the phone back to her face. "Antoinette, can you unload the dishwasher and take out the garbage?"

"Ask Her Royal Highness over there to stop playing with her equations and help out for a change."

Sarah's face suddenly froze and went white as if she'd seen a ghost. Her eyes were glassy, and her mouth was open.

Silence.

The news feeds and the video from Sarah's phone went quiet. Every person in the square had stopped moving and talking. It was as if someone had pressed a pause button on the whole of Sankofa Square. Antoinette played with the controls for the screens, but the feed was live. It wasn't a technical hiccup. Everyone in the square was...*frozen.*

Kris's heart sped up, and she put her hand to her mouth. "Mom, are you okay?" she asked.

"It's like she's asleep. Everyone on all the feeds is stuck," Antoinette said.

As if someone had pressed an invisible play button, the crowd suddenly resumed their actions.

"—stop squabbling and be nice to your sister. I'm so behind on my essay for my class," Sarah said.

"What the hell," Antoinette said. Kris's stomach dropped. She moved closer and sat in front of Sarah's image.

"Do you hear that music?" Sarah asked.

Kris heard it faintly in the background—a sound was emerging in the square. It was almost imperceptible at first, but it was growing louder. The cameras showed people close to the orb clutching their heads as if they had the migraines to end all migraines. Others looked mesmerized, like they were enraptured.

"You were all, like, in a trance or something a minute ago," Antoinette said.

"Mom, get out of there," Kris whispered. She put her hand on the wall over Sarah's face.

Kris had never heard such a sound, but it still was familiar, like someone singing. Where had she heard that voice before? And the orb wasn't black anymore, but glittering with tiny sparkling lights, like a million candles reflecting off a sea of diamonds.

"Do you hear that? The sound is deafening," Kris said. Her heart was beating so fast that she imagined it would burst. The sound made her head hurt.

"I don't see or hear anything. What're you bozos talking about?" Antoinette said.

Without warning, the orb changed color, shifting from the sparkles to a soft red. There was a cry from onlookers filling the square. The news cameras zoomed in, and Sarah's phone shook. The image jerked as Sarah zoomed in on the reddish sphere.

"We're standing here in the middle of downtown Toronto. The mystery orb that came from nowhere is changing from black to red before our eyes," a reporter said, speaking into the jostling camera; the broadcast team found themselves immersed in the crowd.

The sun caught Kris's eyes through the open window, and she blinked. Antoinette knelt on the floor beside her. The two of them sat inches away from Sarah's video feed. Sweat beaded on Antoinette's temples.

"It's like music...coming from the orb," Sarah said.

Kris tried to swallow, but her throat was dry, and she coughed, desperate for water. A multitude of voices filled her head. It started like a child's whisper and grew to a loud roar. She recoiled from the cacophony, though the people around the orb were transfixed by it.

"Get out of there!" Kris screamed, her eyes half closed. Hot tears rolled down her cheeks.

A flash lit up the front window of the Argentia house, like thousands of fireworks going off at once. Kris and Antoinette covered their eyes, blinded by the intensity.

Then silence.

Sarah's link was gone, and the live camera feeds were dead. Loud static filled the air.

"Holy crap," Antoinette muttered.

They ran to the front door to look out toward Toronto. There was no mushroom cloud, like Kris half expected to see, only rustling trees, their old, beat-up Honda Civic in the driveway, and the fat brown cat named Harold walking through the yard.

Kris sank to the ground and rolled into a fetal position with her eyes squeezed shut. The sounds from the orb had stopped, but her head weighed a thousand pounds. Each time she opened her eyes, there was a jolt of raw pain from the brightness coming through the open door. She took deep breaths, and the sensation dissipated.

Kris collected herself and sat by Antoinette in the living room, missing keys as she typed on her phone, trying to reach Sarah. "I can't get hold of her," cried Antoinette. She was in full panic mode. Kris fumbled with the screen controls, searching all the news channels.

No signal...No signal...No signal...

She stopped on one where an in-studio announcer was speaking, her voice quivering.

There was shouting coming from off-camera. The announcer pressed her earpiece in tighter, then typed something into the screen below her on the table. Kris got a chill; no one had any idea what was happening.

"At this point, we can't get a signal from our correspondents on the ground."

breaking news flashed on the bottom of the screen in bright white letters, followed by a replay of footage: people swarming the orb, it turning red, and then the white flash. The drone of static filled the room.

The announcer spoke again, and it sounded surreal to Kris. "We have reports of an incident at the orb. Streaming video showed a flash, then went dead."

Kris opened Rix, but her login page wouldn't pop up. She refreshed the page a few times, but nothing loaded. Other sites weren't opening either. The AI on her phone was down. Traffic had clearly overwhelmed a lot of sites, hitting them like violent ocean waves. No one could send any messages from Toronto.

Antoinette put her head in her hands and let out a long sigh. "Did the orb blow up? We would've heard an explosion; we're not that far from the square. Paula isn't replying to my texts, and she always does, like, right away. I wish someone would say what the hell is going on." There was a look of terror in her eyes.

Kris didn't respond. She closed her eyes, and the world went white. She blocked out the world, focusing on the sounds she'd heard in her head and the pattern of lights she'd studied on the surface of the orb.

"Kris, for Christ's sake, not now. Not one of your goddamn math trances. We have to find Mom." Antoinette's voice was shrill, close to a scream.

Antoinette grabbed Kris's arms and shook her. Kris's eyes snapped open, but she wasn't looking at her sister. Antoinette let her go.

"I understand what it means!" Kris screamed.

She grabbed her diary, charged with a new idea, ran to her room, and closed the door halfway. An idea was brewing in her mind, not as big as the Riemann hypothesis but with more immediate importance. The message contained mathematics, but now she saw that it was a problem.

The music playing in her head confirmed it. The coded message was 100 percent mathematical. She couldn't ignore it.

CHAPTER 3

ERDŐS ALIENS

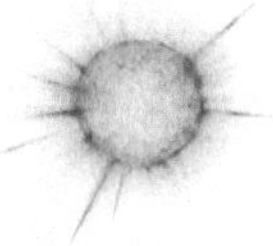

IN A DAZE, Kris watched the brilliant, hot sunshine pour through the window. It had been three and a half hours since the orb appeared and two hours since she had last heard from her mom. The news replayed the same events on an endless loop on the screens in her room. Downtown Toronto was on lockdown, so there were no new images from the scene. There was even a curfew in place, starting that night. Kris spoke with Aunt Tara in Ottawa, who made her promise to heed the authorities and not leave her house.

Everyone who'd been within a certain distance of the orb was *gone*.

The effect had stretched out for over a mile in every direction. Any person in the streets, sitting in an office or a car, walking a dog, or sailing on Lake Ontario had vanished. Cars and bikes crashed as their drivers disappeared. Schoolyards were empty, as were universities and hospitals. City Hall was empty, along with the local news studios that had been buzzing since the appearance of the orb. Cameras lay scattered on the ground, sending images to a baffled audience. The tall office towers in Toronto's financial district, normally abuzz with activity at this hour, were silent.

The intermittent news feed on Rix showed rows of condominium towers along Lake Ontario standing like ominous monoliths.

"Pick up, dammit!" Kris hissed to no one. Sarah was not responding. Kris's face flushed with anger.

She tapped out a text to Nate. Besides Sarah and Antoinette, he was the only one she trusted to help her. He'd texted her soon after the orb had made Sarah and all the others vanish to make sure she was safe. Maybe he would know what to do.

It hadn't taken long for people outside the city to grasp that something was terribly wrong. Further out from downtown, where the vanishing phenomenon had had no effect, people were noticing that their neighbors weren't answering their calls. The boundary of the effect was a clear line, affecting one house or car and not the next. Driverless convoys crawled along the highway shoulders, sensor lights pulsing like erratic heartbeats. There were pileups of cars on every road, empty cars being rear-ended by unsuspecting drivers.

Kris clutched her diary as she watched reports from helicopters flying overhead, several with cameras, beaming images of the silent and empty section of the city to a shocked world. Loss ached in her bones. With Mom gone, what were she and Antoinette supposed to do? All that was left was the two of them.

Kris threw her diary on the ground and lay back on her bed. There was a pain in her chest, and it was difficult to breathe. Her eyes blurred with tears, and her ears were burning hot. She wiped her eyes and nose with her sleeve.

There was a knock. Antoinette walked in and sat on the side of the bed, her face puffy from crying. "Sorry, I yelled at you. I don't know how to deal with all this."

Kris sat up on her bed. She hugged her knees tight.

"Sometimes I think you hate me," Kris said.

"I called Sarah's phone like fifty times. No response. I called nine-one-one and the police. AI isn't working. The lines are all busy. I texted her friends on Rix. They either don't know anything or didn't respond."

"I tried calling her too. And I called Aunt Tara, who said not to leave the house. What're we supposed to do now?"

"No idea. They're not letting anyone near downtown. All the subway lines are closed, along with the roads." Antoinette's voice was calm, but Kris could hear the uncertainty in it.

"I think…" Kris said, her voice trailing off. "I think they're saying hello."

"What? Who is?" Antoinette asked.

"Whoever put the orb there. It's a *greeting*. I can't be sure, but the messages—at least the few I could decipher—are math." Kris pointed to the whiteboard next to her desk, riddled with her calculations.

Antoinette's eyes widened. Kris activated a screen and replayed the first few minutes of the orb's flashes in slow motion. With the speed reduced, it was clear that the dazzling lights formed shapes and had structure. "You see—there? After the snarks? There's this long stretch of blocks, like code. I stared at them for a long time and figured out the cipher. Those blocks are basically the grammar of math. Set theory. The message is sort of a road map to higher math."

"So, lemme get this straight. You're saying a bunch of mathematician terrorists dropped a floating doomsday weapon from nowhere, regurgitated a bunch of set-whatever math, and then vaporized people?" asked Antoinette, looking decidedly unconvinced.

Kris remained serious. "The orb is sending out a message that has a complex mathematical pattern. There are bits about numbers, geometry, and set theory."

Antoinette was right, though. Who would do this? Kris scratched her head and read over her notes. *Could* it be terrorists? Some prank gone wrong?

One of her favorite stories about math was the one the legendary twentieth-century mathematician Paul Erdős had told about Ramsey numbers. It was about how invading aliens came to Earth and demanded to know the value of a certain Ramsey number called R(5). If people couldn't give the precise value of R(5) within a fixed period of time, the aliens said they would destroy the planet. Erdős suggested that people put every computer in the world to work on the problem. His advice if aliens asked for the next unknown value, R(6)? Leave the Earth. The moral of the story was that Ramsey numbers are tough to calculate.

If Kris was right and this situation was similar, then humans were in serious trouble right now. The world would have to work together on this problem before it was too late.

"You know that story I told you about the Erdős aliens invading Earth?" she asked her sister.

"Uh-huh. That Erdős dude was seriously twisted," Antoinette said.

"They're here now. And we don't know the answer to their math problem." Kris felt anxious as she made this admission. There was a mountain of work to do to figure out the solution.

Antoinette's face hardened. Kris knew that look: her sister was going to explode.

She pointed her finger at Kris. "None of this helps us find Sarah. Or Paula or Ryan or Carolyn. Remember them? Our mom? My best friends? They're missing...murdered, as far as we know. And you are sitting here telling me your friggin' math stories!"

Kris teared up again. A familiar panicky sensation welled up: one of two people in the world who loved her unconditionally was *gone*. Antoinette put her head in her hands and let out a sigh.

"I'm sorry," Kris said. "I've texted Nate. He'll know what we should do."

"That asshole only cares about himself," Antoinette muttered. She pushed her bangs back from her face, then slumped over.

Kris's phone vibrated, and she jolted. The news app glowed. She tapped on it, and a screen emerged on the wall. She shuddered when she saw what was happening.

Down in New York, in the middle of Times Square, a second orb appeared. It had come from nowhere, and according to

CCTV feeds, it had elicited screams from those nearby rather than the curiosity roused in Toronto. There was panic. Kris watched vids of the hordes of people scrambling to leave.

"Oh my god," Antoinette said in a whisper.

For a city of so many people, Kris knew ninety minutes wasn't enough time to evacuate. That was the length of time that had passed before the orb in Sankofa Square had detonated. As in Toronto, the New York orb began to light up with complicated mathematical patterns. This time it had no audience as people had fled. The huge screens nearby broadcast their competing messages about the latest shows on Broadway to no one but the orb.

"What does it expect from us?" Kris asked.

She watched the events unfold as if she were paralyzed. The newscaster stumbled over her words as fuzzy satellite images showed taxis and cars in gridlock as congestion on the major routes out of the city built up, clogged with the onslaught of desperate commuters. Hundreds of thousands had already escaped the projected range of the orb, but millions remained trapped in the city. Kris knew the orb was like a ticking time bomb—if the hordes couldn't make it out, they'd vanish like the millions in Toronto had.

The streets of Manhattan looked like a war zone in the afternoon haze. Kris put her hand to her mouth and winced. Anxiety rose in waves from the pit of her stomach. Antoinette's face was white, and neither of them spoke.

Whatever had taken Toronto wasn't done yet, and it was spreading, Kris thought.

Ninety minutes after the second orb showed up, the live video feeds showed it turning black, then red, followed by a flash of light. Kris locked hands with her sister, squeezing tight. Antoinette's hand was cold to the touch.

Toronto's delivery drone lanes had gone pitch dark hours earlier, the sky above Queen Street stripped of its steady buzz. Now the drones above Broadway were similarly grounded, their lanes empty. The city was a ghost town, like Toronto. The Rix reports said millions of New Yorkers were missing.

Kris's phone vibrated again. Another text from Nate:

Stay put. We are on our way to get you.

She typed a response, but it didn't send. Her phone's connection went dead.

Antoinette shot a look at Kris, her eyes all lions and tigers and bears. "Okay, enough of this bullshit. Get your stuff. We're heading downtown to find her."

"The authorities blocked all the ways into downtown. Besides, our car isn't driverless, and you don't have your driver's license!" Kris shouted. Mom hated taking the car downtown, so she took the subway today.

Antoinette said nothing. It wasn't a request to leave but a demand. She was going whether Kris liked it or not.

Kris had too many questions and too few answers. Antoinette pressed the fob of Mom's red gas-guzzling 2027 Honda Civic that was well past its best-before date. The doors unlocked with a click.

Kris folded her arms. "Please don't."

"I've made up my mind," Antoinette said.

"I want to find Mom too, but Nate said he was coming to get us. He said *we*, so maybe he has help with him. Don't you think we should wait a while longer?" Kris said. Antoinette gave her the hairy eyeball.

The low drone of an oncoming car shattered the suburban quiet. A black SUV with blacked-out windows parked behind them, startling Kris and blocking their way out of the driveway. Three people got out. One of them was Nate, but the woman and the tall man dressed in a black suit were unfamiliar.

"Hello, Dr. Argentia. My name is Ajinder Toor. We need to talk," the woman said.

"And who are you?" Antoinette said in a cracking voice, her cheeks turning red as she glared at Toor.

"It's all good, Antoinette. Agent Toor is here to help. Let's all go inside and have a chat," Nate said. The tall, imposing man reached for Antoinette's arm. She shoved him back. He lifted his hands up in a gesture of surrender.

Kris ran to Nate and stopped a foot away from him. "Are you okay?" he asked, his eyes wide and concerned.

The stabbing pain hit her in the chest again, and tears came. "Mom's...Mom's gone."

"It's okay. I'm here now. There is a lot to catch up on."

Antoinette rolled her eyes.

Nate reached out his hand. Surprised by the gesture, Kris took it. He wasn't the touchy-feely type. His hand was warm and gripped hers tightly as they walked inside, the porch door slamming behind them. Even with her mom gone, his grasp anchored her. With both him and Antoinette here, her anxiety about her mom vanishing was close to bearable.

Nate sat at the kitchen table next to Kris and looked at her with a confident smile. Toor and Antoinette stood nearby, glaring daggers at each other.

"If you're wondering whether I understand the message, the answer is no, not yet," Kris said. "I figured out the first part. It looks like they're introducing themselves. Whoever they are. I got past the snarks and primes and into the set theory stuff."

"I saw those bits too. The easy parts. The rest of the message is full of advanced mathematics, much of which makes no sense to me," Nate said.

Toor folded her arms and drew a measured breath. "No doubt you heard about the second orb in New York. Many more are missing. They vanished like the people in Toronto did. All major cities are under evacuation orders."

A chill ran through Kris. Events were happening so fast. A blur within a blur.

"We're facing an unprecedented disaster. We don't know the

purpose of the orbs, but we can say with certainty that they are not from this planet. They are likely the product of a powerful alien intelligence. I'm here on behalf of a group of top government officials to take you to try to communicate with them."

Antoinette stood frozen, disbelief written across her face. Kris avoided Toor's gaze—she was so very direct. Toor's words made the situation more frightening and real.

"Where we're going is safer than your home and most other places in the world right now," Toor added.

"What?" Kris asked.

"A base outside New York City, where we are putting together a team. Think of it as a kind of math think tank. You'll join the others there to decipher the messages."

Images of sitting in a bunker and solving differential equations all day flashed in Kris's brain.

"I'm the team leader," said Nate with a confident smile. He explained that he had collected three other leading math experts to join the team.

"Just use AI. Can't it do almost anything these days?" Antoinette asked.

"Well, not anything. We've tried, and it's not working. We need to leverage the power of the human mind," Nate said.

Kris weighed the options, and none of them were good. If she did nothing, maybe the other mathematicians wouldn't be able to decipher the messages from the orbs. Then Mom would never come back. Even more people could vanish. If she helped Nate, maybe she could find a way to work out the alien message and get Sarah back, but she'd have to leave her home—leave Canada for the first time ever.

All the choices frightened her.

"Hold on. A bunch of James Bond rejects show up at our house, along with Dr. Asshole here, spouting tales about an alien invasion, and you expect us to tag along to your bunker? What happens if we don't go?" Antoinette asked.

Toor stood rigid. "Nothing will happen—at least, not right

away. It's probable that more orbs will appear and that millions more innocent people will vanish. Over time, maybe weeks, or even a month or two, the world as we know it will likely descend into chaos. Governments will dissolve, economies will collapse, and every major city will empty out. There'll be widespread chaos as social systems collapse. It'll be only a matter of time before that affects you directly, I can assure you of that."

"This is a nightmare," Kris said, shuddering.

"Kris, to be blunt, what you've done matters. You're one of the few people who can help us think through this. If you're willing to work with Dr. Wallace and his team, we have a better chance of understanding the patterns and figuring out how to respond. We'll keep you safe, and we'll make sure you have what you need to work."

"They're Erdős aliens," Kris said.

"Pardon me?" asked Toor.

Nate grinned.

"The aliens in Erdős's story—they're who we must be dealing with. The ones who come to Earth with a mathematical question. If we can't answer the question, then we're finished."

Toor was silent, her face betraying no emotion. It was like looking at an android.

"Who are you people? CSIS? CIA?" Antoinette asked.

"None and both of the above. I represent a conglomerate of world intelligence agencies charged with meeting this hostile alien invasion."

Kris mulled these words over, rolling them around in her brain. *How come we've never heard anything about them until now?*

"We'll think about your offer and call you tomorrow," Antoinette said.

"My apologies, but we need your answer *now*. As we mentioned, we're preparing to fly to an undisclosed location outside New York City and will join the team of experts there."

"What about Mom?" Kris asked.

Nate jumped in. "We don't know what happened to Sarah or

the others. The orbs left the cities intact. Only the people are gone. She may still be alive." The small pause before his last few words betrayed him. It was a fragile hope, and Kris could see through it.

Antoinette exploded. "Are you kidding me? You think Sarah's safe? She just *vanished*?"

Toor's voice softened. "I lost people to the orbs too. But I don't believe they came here to destroy us."

Nate leaned forward, steadying himself on the table. "Our plan is the best chance we have of bringing her back."

Kris didn't know what was true anymore.

"All you've ever cared about is yourself. Don't pretend to be so concerned about my kid sister," Antoinette said. The remark got under his skin; he pursed his lips. Kris's stomach performed Olympic-worthy somersaults. Nate and Antoinette never got along since the moment they met.

Antoinette let out a long sigh. "If it were up to me, we would leave you here and go search for Sarah downtown."

"There's nothing for you to do downtown. The two of you will be much safer under our protection. We wouldn't be asking this if the situation wasn't so dire, but we need to act quickly. Look at what happened in Manhattan. You'll agree the situation is critical. We've seen two orbs on Earth now, and it's possible more will appear," Toor said.

She'd said "on Earth." Kris was suspicious. Toor knew more than she was saying. Why were the orbs here now? Why Toronto and New York City?

The mood was tense as Toor and Antoinette continued to glare at each other. Antoinette was terrified by the prospect of Kris joining this team.

That alien message was complex, maybe even beyond Kris's ability to understand. The whole thing could be a pointless—even dangerous—waste of time. But it might also be her one chance to save her mom, if Nate was right about her being alive.

What if she didn't help and more orbs popped up? The same

nauseous feeling she'd had earlier came back, but she struggled to push it away. She had to *try*, didn't she? After all, a mathematician wasn't usually offered a chance to play the heroine.

Kris broke the awkward silence. "I'll do it," she said. "I don't know if it's the right thing. I don't even know if it'll work. But I can't just sit here and do nothing. I need to at least try."

Antoinette was about to say something, but Kris got up and grabbed her hands. "This is our best chance to get Mom back." Kris figured they would be safer with Toor and Nate than on their own.

Toor let a hint of a smile show. "Good. Bring only essentials. We will get you everything else you need."

Kris grabbed her $f(u)=c^k$ mug. "You'll be working on math, so don't forget your notebook," Antoinette said.

"I could never forget my little black book," Kris said. Her diary lay on her dresser, and she put it in her knapsack. It was her most prized possession.

She and Antoinette found two of Sarah's suitcases. One was larger and black, the other small and red. The red one had a tag on it from Sarah's last visit to her sister, Tara, which reminded Kris to return her aunt's latest texts. They loaded each with clothes and toiletries. Each thing Kris put in made her heart heavier. Finally, Kris grabbed her knapsack, and Antoinette picked up her old guitar case covered in stickers.

"All right. Let's move," Toor said.

"Before we go, do you know what's going on in other cities? My Rix feed just died," Kris asked Toor.

Toor's back straightened. "The major cities all around the world are under evacuation, and urban dwellers are pouring into the surrounding rural areas. Governments are racing to set up relocation camps outside the urban centers."

The vision overwhelmed Kris. All those people would soon be living in tents, in strange places away from their homes. She pictured millions moving in endless lines, the highways clogged with abandoned cars, and knew Toor's clinical words barely scratched the surface of the chaos. Most people now were or would soon be refugees. Doctors, scientists, lawyers, and teachers. Kids, adults, and the elderly.

Kris's hands shook.

"The crowding in the relocation camps will create a humanitarian crisis. Access to essentials like food, water, shelter, and medicine will become a problem everywhere. London, Delhi, Paris, Los Angeles—the list of cities under evacuation keeps growing. People have barely begun to move, yet panic is spreading and nations are moving troops," Toor said.

It was ten minutes before six p.m. when they piled into the car. Kris looked back at her home through the tinted window. The house was small, modest. But it was home, her only one. She might never see it again. Sadness took her, and she held her head in her hands. For a brief moment, she saw Sarah standing in the window, looking out at her as they sped away. It was as if she were leaving her mother forever.

They drove along the empty highways to Pearson Airport, which was now under military control. After being greeted by several men in fatigues, they boarded a jet. As Kris took her seat, she discovered that Toor's team was staring at her. She tried to ignore them, but one of the agents came over to talk to them. He was a tall, muscular African American man, around six-foot-three, who identified himself as Agent Elliott Diya. He was the agent who came to their house.

"We have clearance to land at JFK. After that, we'll go to a base where you'll have a chance to sleep. Then tomorrow morning there'll be a debrief and a press conference led by Toor and Wallace."

"Press conference? Dear lord," Kris said under her breath.

"Don't worry," Diya continued. "You won't have to say anything. We're going public with our plans to help ease the global panic. After that, you can begin your work."

The idea of it made Kris despair. She remembered the reporters and photographers outside the university on the day of her doctoral defense. They'd announced on the news that she'd proven the Collatz conjecture in her doctoral thesis weeks earlier. One of the reporters in the crowd had stepped on Antoinette's foot, and she'd sworn and grabbed him by the arm. She was lucky that nobody had pressed charges.

The doctoral committee grilled me for hours. They doubted me. Even now, big-name mathematicians were writing articles picking apart my proof. But I know it's right, Kris thought.

Sarah refused to let Kris do any interviews except one to Scientific American. Kris had explained the conjecture to the young reporter on Rix: "Start with a positive integer. If the number is even, then divide it by two. If the number is odd, then multiply it by three and add one. Repeat over and over. If you keep repeating, eventually, you get one. For example, start with three. Then you get ten, five, sixteen, eight, four, two, and then one. Bang!" She'd then proceeded to sketch her proof over the next hour, filling the screen while the reporter ran out of questions.

The conjecture was much simpler to state than to prove.

Diya cleared his throat, and Kris snapped back to the present. "We're going to introduce you and the other members of the mathematics team to the press," he said.

"Of course. Call us the M-Team," Kris said. "I like that. It has a nice ring to it."

CHAPTER 4

THE M-TEAM

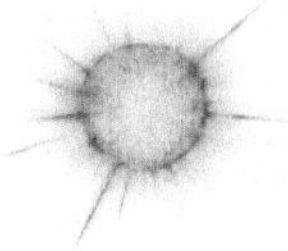

K RIS HAD FLOWN only once in her life, and that had been a short trip to Ottawa for her aunt's wedding. She remembered the forty-five-minute journey from the Toronto Island Airport well. It was odd to deplane now and see soldiers rather than duty-free shops. The airports in New York City and Toronto remained under total military control.

Two black SUVs, identical to the ones in Toronto, sat on the tarmac alongside the plane in the hazy late evening. They piled into those. The fake leather seats were hot and sticky against Kris's legs. They pushed north from JFK through highways frozen with abandoned cars, driving on the shoulder and threading through gaps left by fleeing drivers, and hours later reached a military base north of the city. Armed guards let them through the barricade, revealing a microcity containing dozens of people bustling around like worker ants. Kris soaked in the sprawling complex.

On the way there, Nate gave Kris a tablet with information about the base. It sat in the countryside amid farms and wandering cattle. A repurposed warehouse was the home of his mathematical think tank. The team would work here to decode the alien message using state-of-the-art computing. Inside the warehouse, a secure lab ran machines that combined quantum cores with ordinary processors, the kind of power that hadn't even existed when she was a kid.

Nate had handpicked four of the top living mathematicians for the team, each working in different fields of cutting-edge research. These individuals represented the brightest and boldest minds in the field of mathematics. There were sleeping quarters on the premises for more than thirty soldiers and other assorted personnel. The lower-ranked members of the military crammed together with bunk beds, while members of the mathematics team had private rooms. There was a mess hall to feed them and offices for Toor and Nate.

At the heart of it all was the M-Team workroom. It was there that the mathematicians would toil away. Four white, windowless walls enclosed the room; three held screens and whiteboards. There were minimalist desks with a chair behind each—comfortable, but not overly so. This nerve center would be supported by secondary and tertiary groups composed of statisticians, linguists, and computer scientists in secure, undisclosed locations. Kris skipped over the part about quantum algorithms and deep learning on Nate's tablet, and the rest read like gibberish.

Kris marveled at how this had come together in such a short period of time. It had been less than one day since the incident in Sankofa Square. The base was clearly intended for another purpose. The smells of sawdust and Pine-Sol lingered.

Her quarters were bare, white, and minimalist. She dropped her bags and fell onto the bed, yawning and stretching. The place might have been austere, but it had what she needed: space to think without distractions, a computer with a projectable screen, a desk and swivel chair, a small bed, and a wardrobe. Her phone couldn't connect to the internet, and the computer could only get into the base's files. A restroom with clean white tiles connected to Antoinette's quarters next door. In times like these, it was extra nice being close to her.

Kris took the framed photo of Sarah from her bag, brushed her thumb over her face once, and set it on the small table beside her bed. A sudden worry surfaced. She could lose Sarah before she saw her again. She pushed it away.

She then took a glossy page from her bag and pinned it with a tack she'd brought to the wall over her bed: a photo from an old-fashioned print magazine of ETC in all his lovely K-pop glory.

He'd been her first crush. She was a big fan even now, but not as diehard as she'd been years ago. He was so handsome, tall and thin, with long lashes and black wavy hair. She'd signed up for every fan page on Rix and had even convinced Sarah to take her to see his sold-out concert. Although he'd looked like an ant from their cheap seats, he'd loomed larger than life on the screens in the stadium. When he'd waved in her direction, her heart had stopped. The image was silly, childish even, but it reminded her of home.

Tuesday, July 17, 2035. Imagine a movie where aliens abduct your mom and two million other people. Then the heroine has to figure out a way to get them back with...math. That's my life right now, Kris penned in her diary.

Agent Diya knocked on her door to collect her at seven in the morning. Her eyelids were heavy as boulders.

"Where are we going now?" Kris asked, yawning.

"You'll be debriefed on the classified intelligence we have about the orb first," Diya said.

"Okay, but can I have a coffee first?" Kris asked. She cleaned up as best she could without the luxury of a shower, then followed him. Antoinette joined Kris and wanted to attend the meeting, but Toor, who was waiting for Kris in the lobby area outside the workroom, vetoed it.

"You've got to be joking. Aren't I her legal guardian now?" Antoinette said to Toor.

Kris put a hand on her sister's shoulder. "Ant, please don't make a scene."

"I just don't get it," Antoinette muttered. "All those years you skipped—did they really make you smarter?"

Kris stepped into the cavernous meeting space, where Toor and Nate sat at a round table along with military and intelligence personnel, a mix of older men and a few women wearing uniforms with shiny insignias. There were well-known mathematicians sprinkled in between them—at least, well-known to Kris. One of them, an older woman who looked familiar, glanced her way, and she suddenly had to stop herself from sinking lower in her chair. The table surface lit as she approached, its AI sketching her personal ID in faint lines of blue.

The sight of these people intimidated her, making her feel small and out of place. She shook Nate's hand but avoided his gaze. He patted her hand and offered a hint of a smile, then resumed his seat next to Toor.

A screen popped up on the wall, and Toor stood tall and commanding next to it. Kris's stomach tightened; the space was more like a courtroom than a classroom, and it felt like she was the one on trial.

"Good morning. Now that Dr. Argentia has joined us, I'd like to begin. What you're about to hear is highly classified intelligence gathered by various groups over the last few months."

The screen showed an ochre-hued, rocky wasteland with mountains in the distance under a hazy orange sky. A gray robotic arm was in the center of the screen. NASA's rovers ran on ordinary hardware because the advanced quantum processors weren't ready for Mars. The picture progressed in slow motion, as if it were underwater. Video from a mounted camera on a rover moved at a snail's pace across the desert landscape.

It looked like something out of a movie, but this was real life, real science; these were images from the Mars Johnson IV mission, the rover that had been lost weeks ago after a violent dust storm. The rover was named after one of Kris's favorite mathematicians, the late great Katherine Johnson. Several of the world's space agencies had sent probes to Mars over the last few decades to study its geology and look for signs of primitive life. Given the distance from the Earth, robots were a cheaper way to study the neighboring planet. NASA's recent mission to the Valles Marineris canyon had been looking for signs of microbial life. Many scientists believed such life could exist in the canyon filled with water vapor. They'd hoped to find the first sign of life off Earth, although no one had expected to find sentient life.

The scene cut to a different red, rocky landscape, but this time there was a black dot on the horizon. The robot started its long journey toward the dot. Toor moved the video forward such that the rover progressed a few hundred feet. In the distance, the canyon was dark and foreboding.

That round black shape—it was an orb, identical to the ones in Toronto and New York. An orb on another planet. Kris remembered half-baked conspiracy threads about the Mars mission, posts she'd dismissed at the time.

"The incident in Toronto wasn't our first encounter with an orb," said Toor. "It was during the Johnson IV's mission that we first detected one. That was ten weeks ago. We're not sure why the aliens attempted to make first contact with one of our probes on Mars rather than come to Earth. Perhaps it was a preemptive move to determine our capacity for communication before invading our world, as they've done now in Toronto and New York. To avoid panic, we kept the incident from the public and falsely reported that the rover was lost in a Martian dust storm."

The screen showed a familiar set of patterns appearing on the orb's surface. The sight of an orb flashing mathematics on Mars made Kris shudder. Toor had known about it but hadn't told anyone, at least anyone without clearance. Creepy. Kris wanted to run out of the room but couldn't move.

Toor continued. "It should be clear to you by now that these orbs are extraterrestrial. Experts in linguistics worked for weeks, but they managed to decipher only a fraction of the patterns on the orb. This orb didn't act hostile, unlike the ones here on Earth. This may be due to the absence of humanoid life forms. We don't know. With the rover, it displayed its patterns in a loop, repeating them every two hours. We've digitized the message for you to see."

The room went dark, and the screen went black. A complex set of patterns popped up—the ones from the orbs, but flattened out. The space flickered with a dazzling display of black-and-white images, like fireflies swimming in the summer sky. The patterns blinked far too fast for the human eye to make sense of them.

"It's mathematics. Alien math, if you will," Toor said.

It's so beautiful, Kris thought. Her mind reeled at the complexity of it, like when she'd finished her proof of the Riemann hypothesis. She put her hand to her mouth, transfixed by the light show.

"This is clearly a message from a sentient alien life form. It's directed toward humans specifically. Our best linguists and cryptologists, armed with the most powerful quantum-powered AI, cannot make sense of it. We think this is a mathematical test of our ability to communicate with them."

People muttered. Kris bit her lip as she watched this information sink in. The orbs were, without a doubt, from the Erdős aliens.

"What happens if we fail the test?" she said amid the buzzing chatter. Patronizing smiles and curious looks met her question.

"We don't know the answer to that question, Dr. Argentia, but based on recent events, it's clear that this won't end well for us. The evacuations of our largest urban centers are creating a humanitarian disaster of historic proportions. The world's governments can't maintain law and order under these circumstances for much longer. The situation is already becoming dire. I give us a few weeks, tops, before our civilization undergoes complete collapse."

They kept saying how bad it was, but no one was talking about how to fix it, Kris thought. She decided it was best not to ask Toor any more questions for now.

More buzzing.

"Fortunately for us, we do have a plan, which brings us to our guests today. With the help of Dr. Nathaniel Wallace, we've brought the world's best mathematical minds together to work on deciphering the spheres' patterns and communicating with the aliens. He has been working tirelessly to unravel the alien message since our first encounter with the orb on Mars. As most of you know, Dr. Wallace is one of the world's leading mathematicians, a Fields medalist, the chair of the mathematical sciences division at the National Science Foundation, and a special scientific advisor to the President. He also holds an endowed professorship in Toronto, where he supervised another of our team, Dr. Kris Argentia. With that, I give the floor to him."

Nate walked to the podium. His body language was what Kris expected. His chin was up and his chest out. He loved the attention and was squarely in his element. Nate was confident and well-dressed. He was the polished person she wanted to become.

Nate explained that their goal was simple: find a way to communicate with the orbs, stop their proliferation, and bring back Earth's missing citizens. He introduced the four members of the team, giving a brief biography of each person and a summary of their expertise. Luke Wheeler from Boston was the world's leading expert on number theory. Lara Armistead from Paris was an expert in functional analysis and the geometry of infinite-dimensional spaces. She'd only seen Lara in pictures on Rix.

Just wow. Lara is here. I'm totally fangirling right now, Kris thought.

Benedita Carvalho, the expert in algebra from Brazil, nodded at Kris; she looked to be in her twenties, closest to Kris's age. She had the most beautiful ebony skin, and her hair was like long, springy coils. From Nate's summaries, which were on Kris's tablet, these were the cream of the crop.

"The youngest member of our team is Kris Argentia from Toronto. Kris is well known to many of you as a child prodigy in mathematics and has proven many long-standing mathematical conjectures in her brief career, including tackling the famous Collatz problem in her doctoral thesis, which she defended earlier this year. Kris is an expert in many areas of mathematics, including combinatorics and number theory."

Every face turned toward her. Kris lowered her eyes. The attention felt uncomfortable, like standing too close to a bright light. She turned the pen in her fingers and let it wander across the page, drawing without thinking so she wouldn't have to look up. She was grateful when the discussion moved on.

Toor had chosen the base as the central location for operations with the blessings of the US government and intelligence officials. Nate described the workroom in the base that would be the nerve center for mathematical research. The team would work together to crack the aliens' message. The job of the secondary and tertiary teams was to interface with supercomputing clusters around the world. The M-Team had the tough work: they would be the front line, grappling with the message.

The military brass, led by Nate and Toor, applauded. They were like caricatures to Kris, sitting there in their uniforms and regalia.

She was uncertain of how this team—the M-Team—would be able to work together to find a solution. Kris had only collaborated with Nate and one other mathematician in her life: Cynthia Tran, who'd visited the university months ago. Her experience researching with Cynthia gave her a sliver of hope. Kris grinned as she remembered the final night of Cynthia's stay, when they'd completed a marathon math session that had lasted until midnight. Cynthia looked ancient, in her late fifties, with short, gray hair and hands made leathery by the sun. Kris had scratched out the final line of their proof on the blackboard and let out a whoop. Cynthia's smile had shone like the sun on a cloudless July day.

Toor spoke again with her characteristic cold confidence. "Thank you, Dr. Wallace. Now that we've completed our introductions, the next step is to have a press conference. The public needs to hear about our efforts, which will help slow the panic that's ensuing out there."

As the participants stood, Kris raised her hand. The military types scowled. They didn't appreciate her curiosity. They were more used to giving orders than fielding questions from a teenager.

"Yes, Dr. Argentia? What's your question?" Toor asked.

"Um, you want us to decode the alien message—I get that part. But then what? How will we respond if we figure out what it means?"

Nate replied in a haughty tone. "Once we understand their message, it'll likely become apparent how we should respond. We're assuming that any alien intelligence that can travel vast distances between stars and communicate using advanced mathematics would have the capacity for restraint. Once we can answer them, they should stop their hostile actions against us. Besides, I'll be leading the M-Team. We'll find a way under my guidance," he said with supreme confidence.

Kris never knew which Nate she would get. Mentor or performer.

"What if we don't have the answers they're looking for? I mean, what could go wrong with tinkering with the alien orbs?"

Toor jumped in, her face betraying not a hint of emotion. "We've addressed that point already. We need to move on now. The meeting is closed."

Kris hated that they were treating her like a child. They were dismissing her points without even considering them. Toor, Nate, and the others in their entourage left.

All of it only mattered if it helped bring her mom back, Kris thought.

Kris met Antoinette in the lobby area outside. "I might get in trouble for telling you. We're going to try to communicate with the aliens, just like we discussed earlier."

"Like the Erdős story."

"Yeah, like in the story. We have to find a way to communicate with these orbs before more people vanish."

"Kris, something's bugging me. Why do you think the aliens chose to speak in math? Why not use English? Or they could speak in art, or dance, or colors."

Kris shrugged. "I don't think anyone knows. I guess it's because mathematics is the basic language of the universe. Take the number pi, for example."

A quizzical look spread across Antoinette's face. She waited for her to get to the point.

Kris continued. "We have languages and history and art. But aliens wouldn't, at least not the same way. They may not have music or paintings."

"What does this have to do with anything?" Antoinette asked.

Kris continued. "Their bodies could be totally different from ours. But mathematics is universal. Like, if you take a circle with radius one, then the area of it is pi. That's true here, and it's true in every other galaxy, whether you have eight fingers or ten. Or none. I don't know. We can't know if a Warhol painting or a Joan Jett song would mean the same thing to them as it does to us."

Kris's explanation wasn't helping. "They killed millions, for Christ's sake. How can you talk about pi and alien fingers?" Antoinette asked.

"They may not even have noticed," Kris said. "I don't think they even see things the way we do."

"Say that again?"

"I mean that to the aliens, we may seem so small that making a few million of us vanish wouldn't seem too important. They are waiting for our response, I think," Kris said.

"But...what should the response be? As far as we know, they only speak in math patterns."

"Then we'll make mathematical patterns of our own!" Kris exclaimed.

◎ ∘ ◎

Kris walked down the long white hallways of the base like a ghost with no home. There was nothing on the walls other than paint, tubes, and wires. While the building was finished, the construction crews had rushed in places: parts of the walls were unpainted, and she spotted some missing ceiling tiles and switch plates.

The place gave her the heebie-jeebies.

She entered a larger space with long rows of tables and chairs. The place had a chemical smell like bleach. There was a cafeteria at the back. A teenage boy was there, sitting by himself and writing something on a pad of paper with a black pen.

The boy lifted his face.

"Hello," Kris said.

"Yo," he responded. A curious light shone from his eyes.

He wore a simple white V-neck T-shirt and shorts. She tried not to stare at the few black chest hairs sticking out of his shirt. Kris walked forward, and the mathematics he was writing caught her eye. She sat next to him.

"Those are interesting equations. Diophantine ones?" Kris asked.

"Uh-huh. I'm teaching myself this kind of math since the stuff we do in high school is so boring. I'm at the top of my class back in D.C."

Kris bit her lip. He sounded cocky like Nate.

She scanned his work. "Systems of linear Diophantine equations, and you're using the Smith method to solve them. Cool. Have you learned about elliptic curves yet?"

He shook his head, looking surprised that this interloper had dropped in on his calculations.

"Here, let me show you." She opened a screen on the table with her phone, and handwritten equations were scrawled on it. She walked him through her notes outlining a new method of finding integral points on elliptic curves. His dark eyes bulged as he stared at her calculations.

"What is that? Wait a minute—you're Kris Argentia, aren't you?"

"Yes."

"I'm Ari. My mom is Ajinder Toor."

Kris coughed. The base wasn't supposed to have teens, except her and Antoinette, and Ari was there under different rules. She had no idea Toor had a son, let alone a cute one. Not pop star, ETC-level cute, of course. Ari had jet-black hair and a dark complexion. His ears stuck out a little.

"I was visiting Uncle Ravi on Long Island when the orb appeared in Toronto. Mom was in Houston visiting NASA, and she flew to New York after the orb showed up there. What a disaster, and not even that far from us. People going to camps and all that. Mom had a bad feeling about the orbs even before they made people disappear. But she doesn't talk about her work with me. The top-secret CIA-type stuff."

"So you're not part of the M-Team, then?"

"I'm no mathematician. I love math, but that's not the same thing, I guess," Ari said.

"You can keep my sister company. Her name's Antoinette. I mean, she isn't a mathematician either."

Ari shrugged.

"Um, so...I've got to go to the press conference now," Kris said.

"Nice to meet you, Doc Kris with the golden hair," he said.

Kris's heart beat faster.

The chatter of reporters packed shoulder to shoulder rose in a dull roar. They had come from every major news outlet, been flown in or driven to the base by Toor's agents. The afternoon press conference was underway. Heat pressed down on the cramped space, and the air conditioning was throttled back to conserve power. Kris shifted uncomfortably; the spotlights made her skin itch, and she wiped the sweat from her brow. She sat with the M-Team behind a table near the lectern, just out of reach of the microphones, close enough to be seen but not yet heard.

"Let the circus begin," she whispered to herself.

Toor's spokesperson addressed the media. He was tall, with short, sandy-blond hair and brown eyes. He wore a dark blue suit and tie. Attractive, non-threatening.

"We're asking people not to panic," he said.

A torrent of questions poured from the reporters. All cameras pointed at the podium.

"How can you ask that when a million or more are dead or missing?" said someone in the front row.

"We don't know where the vanished people are. But we've contained the *objects*, and there is every indication that this incident will remain isolated in two cities—Toronto and New York City."

There was another flurry of questions, but one broke through. "Can you describe the timeline of what happened in Sankofa Square?"

"Our reports show that at ten fourteen a.m. on Monday morning, the orb appeared. It began flashing patterns of white lights soon after that. At eleven forty-five a.m., enhanced satellite images and video feeds from the incident showed the same thing. The patterns stopped, and the orb changed color. There was a white flash. After that, we lost touch with every person in approximately a mile radius around the orb. Similar events occurred in New York City at three twenty p.m., with the epicenter in Times Square."

More questions.

"But are they dead? Are the people who vanished in Toronto and New York *dead*?"

The spokesperson cleared his throat. "We hope that they're safe and will be returned to us in the near future."

"But what is the orb? What are the patterns flashing on it? Is it a form of communication?" asked one reporter.

"Is it a warning? Or an ultimatum?" asked another.

Kris's heart pounded. Was he going to tell them the truth, share the knowledge that they were not alone in the cosmos?

There was a long pause. Then the spokesperson said, "We are certain—as certain as we can be—that the orb *isn't terrestrial* in origin. Furthermore, we believe that the orb is trying to communicate with us through mathematics."

The chatter grew to a loud roar; there was shouting, even pushing. Reporters had their phones out, and every camera focused on the spokesperson. Some journalists furiously typed on their screens while others clamored for the attention of the spokesperson.

"We cannot comment further, as the subject is classified. We're doing everything in our power to return the victims to their loved ones. We have our best people working on this problem."

There were more questions and more shouting. One caught the attention of everyone.

"Are you saying the orb was made by *aliens*? From outer space?"

Raising his hand to quell the din, the spokesperson said, "Yes." The press erupted into shouts again.

"We'll now hear from the director of mathematical operations, Dr. Nathaniel Wallace."

Nate stepped to the podium. The room slowly settled as he began to speak, laying out the plan to reach the aliens in careful, measured terms. He introduced each of the mathematicians on the M-Team. Kris was not used to this much attention but went along with it. Toor had said that seeing them would make the public less panicked.

There were many more questions. Reporters asked about the location of the President. She and all other world leaders were safe, and she'd be addressing the nation and the world from an undisclosed location that evening. Someone asked if a military strike against the aliens was an option.

"That could backfire. Attacking the orbs would antagonize them further and could result in the loss of many more people," Nate said.

Reporters asked the members of the M-Team for their comments on the situation. Kris broke into a cold sweat and wondered what she should say. Maybe she should talk about Erdős? Everyone loved her Erdős stories.

When it was her turn, the flashes of cameras startled her, and she squinted into the bright lights. The press was silent. Struck by a sudden wave of shyness, she looked down, then up at the gaggle of expectant reporters. Her hands trembled. She reached over to pull the microphone closer and knocked over a tall glass of water, sending rivulets across the table. She grabbed her diary before it got soaked and blotted at the mess with loose papers. Nate's eyes narrowed as two of the reporters in the front row laughed.

"Sorry, I'm such a klutz. My name's Kris and…I'm here to help," she said to the cameras, her cheeks hot.

"That's the math prodigy, Kris Argentia," whispered one reporter to another. "She's the smartest in the bunch."

Oh, $f(u)=c^k$.

Kris was high on adrenaline when the press conference ended. She also felt the weight of the task before her. She had to do this. She *needed* to get Sarah back. The whole world depended on her.

The cold white corridors were no comfort to her as she walked down them. She had to speak to Antoinette. She knocked on her door.

"It's open," Antoinette said, and Kris shuffled in. The barren white space had a single bed, like hers, and blank screens splashed across the walls like graffiti.

"How did it go? I've still got no connection."

Kris plopped down on the bed. Her heart sank. "That was bananas," she said. The possibility of this becoming a global disaster came into vivid focus. It terrified her. No more cities. No more civilization.

"Aunt Tara texted. She's safe but stuck in a camp outside Ottawa. Rix is super spotty so we may not hear from her in a while."

"Oh crap," Kris said.

"I know you'll solve the problem. You have to."

They hugged, and Kris lay her head on Antoinette's shoulder.

"Do you think Mom's dead?" Kris asked.

She could feel her sister's muscles clenching as she said, "No way."

Quiet at last.

The evening was humid, but the vent above her bed was blowing delicious cool air over her head. Kris was alone, staring at her diary, curled up with a blanket on her bed. Her diary was a comfort to her. It was a silent friend to whom she could tell anything.

She should have been sleeping, but she studied the patterns on the orb one more time. The sequence of patterns was playing in slow motion on a screen. It was the one light in the space, and it flickered across her page. Her pen cast dancing shadows there.

Her racing thoughts kept her awake. *Let's apply logical thinking to this problem.*

An alien race had presented Earth with a complex mathematical message. Carl Sagan would approve.

The mathematicians had no trouble deciphering the first minute or so of the message. The rest were meaningless patterns. Kris opened a second screen and accessed the data-mining software the statistics cohort had created for the M-Team. Oceans of code popped up, which Kris navigated with the menu tree.

Teams across the globe were applying sophisticated algorithms to the message. Though there were many bright ideas from big data and artificial intelligence, people had used every linguistic and cryptologic method to analyze the data with no success. Kris knew that this wasn't a simple code to break. They needed more than a cipher. They needed to understand the underlying mathematics in the torrent of patterns.

Her ears were hot; that was how she knew she was on to something. This was an alien test.

Of course, the Erdős–Ramsey number story, she thought.

What about *Ramsey theory*? If you scanned a clear night sky with no light pollution, you could see thousands of stars with the naked eye. If you stared long enough, you would see patterns. The constellations were like that—the result of human minds projecting their ideas about the universe onto a bunch of lights in random positions in the sky. What if the same principle applied to the alien message?

Kris brought up the message again but projected it into three-dimensional space by throwing in an axis for time. She pulled up an algorithm for combinatorial pattern matching. Menu tree alpha, submenu gamma...

Her jaw dropped at the result.

The message had a *shape*! It had a clear beginning, several fluctuations in the middle, and then an ending. Not only that, but the whole thing had a high degree of symmetry. If she played it backward, it was similar to when she played it forward. Kris moved the plot around and split it down the middle. She then separated the two halves; they were similar but different. One wasn't a mirror image of the other. When she used the pattern-matching algorithm and a Fourier transform to reduce the noise, a much clearer picture emerged. Menu tree beta, submenu epsilon...

The message could be divided cleanly into ten distinct parts, each with a beginning, a middle, and an end. The first part she'd mastered, so she tried the second. It too had ten parts, each with a similar structure to the larger message.

Ten fingers, ten toes. Kris bit her lip.

While she couldn't understand the details of the message, this was a breakthrough in deciphering it. She saved her results and emailed them to Nate and the other members of the M-Team.

There was one more thing she had to do before sleeping.

Kris opened her phone and tapped on a folder called Gal Pals, her made-from-scratch hacking software. With it, she might be able to hack into Toor's files through the base's local network. A screen popped up on the wall, and she navigated through half a dozen menus, entering passwords and iris scans.

Computers were so logical. Pure randomness drove the brains of humans. Even the way her own mind worked puzzled her—sometimes she'd be stuck for days on a math problem, and then the answer would pop into her head when she was watering a plant or clipping her toenails.

Computers were different from humans in many ways. They were brilliant idiots, Nate would call them. Lightning fast but lacking that spark of ingenuity that humans once thought was uniquely theirs. They spoke in precise languages. And luckily for her, many of those languages were mathematical. And math was her *specialty*.

There was a pulsing red dot on the screen. Kris hesitated, her finger trembling. She drew a deep breath and pressed it. A login prompt flashed, glowing white against a blue background. It was the Rix login of Agent Ajinder Toor. She wanted to do a happy dance.

"If she finds out, I'm a goner," Kris muttered.

Her hacking software tried 44,586,000,000-character combinations in the password field in a few seconds. She'd disabled the security protocol that allowed her to try only three passwords before it locked up. And also, the bit about needing Toor's iris scan; that wouldn't do at all.

Kris loved Gal Pals. She'd written the code from scratch when she was fourteen. Sarah hadn't been happy when she'd caught Kris reading hacking how-tos tucked away in the darker parts of Rix. But Gal Pals let her listen in when Nate complained to the department head about Kris being late for his seminars. It let her eavesdrop on her mom when she'd started seeing that guy from her English course. That had been too gross, though, so she didn't read Sarah's channels anymore.

Kris trusted Nate. But Toor was all secret and aloof. How come everyone did everything she asked without question? Who were all the other agents? She had to know more; it could help her get her mom back quicker.

The screen flashed three times. Kris sighed with relief and cracked her knuckles.

She was in.

She smiled so widely it was like she'd been delivered a double-chocolate sundae. As always, Gal Pals worked like a charm. She shredded her history files and cleared the event logs, making it impossible for anyone to know she was there. Now that she knew she could get in without detection, she would come back later and search for answers.

Kris glanced at the clock and yawned. Her head ached, and her back was sore from sitting in one position for so long. In the dim light, ETC's smile beamed from the photo pinned to the wall. She moved off the bed, and a heavy book fell to the floor with a thud. There was a knock on her side of the bathroom door. It was Antoinette.

"For God's sake, K, have you been up long? It's almost morning."

"I didn't sleep at all. I was working on math."

Her stomach growled as she admitted to herself that the knot in her stomach was hunger. Tonight wasn't her first all-nighter, and it wouldn't be her last.

CHAPTER 5

THE MAKER

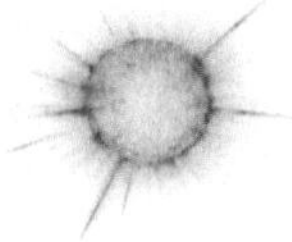

K RIS'S MIND RACED *as she gazed at the patterns. She and the orb faced each other in Toronto in an otherwise empty Sankofa Square.*

"What do you want?" Kris asked.

She didn't expect an answer. The white flashes continued flickering over the surface of the orb, undeterred by her presence. Kris concentrated. She heard a sound like a whistling wind, growing in intensity until it became a dull roar. No, it wasn't the wind, she concluded.

It was the music.

The music she'd heard her whole life, the kind she'd heard when she'd done her first proof at the age of ten and again when she'd proven the Riemann hypothesis. Her body locked up with fear as the voices rose and uttered the word:

"Maker."

Kris opened her eyes and was back in her bed at the base. With no windows to let in natural light, the place was dark. She could make out the white walls in the soft glow of her phone. The music had been a dream. The sound of those voices, thin and shaky, echoed inside her. The sensation was fleeting but unsettling. If she was quiet, she could still hear them speaking.

She fumbled for her phone on the table beside the bed. Eight a.m. on Wednesday morning. Two whole days had passed since the orbs had come and Sarah had gone missing.

One conclusion forced its way forward, as unavoidable as a proof: she had to visit an orb. As soon as possible.

But how? It would have to be Times Square, since that was the closest one. Kris didn't know the next time she'd visit Toronto. She knew Nate wouldn't allow her to investigate an orb close up, and neither would Toor. That left one person she could trust, one person who would help her get to an orb. Then she could talk to it and get Mom back.

Guards surrounded Times Square, looking for anything unusual. And worse, Kris was on a military base miles from Manhattan. She was surrounded by soldiers watching her every move. There was no easy way for her to access an orb. But that didn't mean it was impossible. And difficulty had never stopped her before.

Kris got out of bed and scratched her neck. She opened a screen, tapped on Gal Pals, and hacked into Toor's Rix interface again to gain access to the sites she needed. She put her head in her hands and yawned. She was so groggy that she struggled to keep her eyes open.

Even if she could get off the base, how would she get down to New York City? She couldn't drive, and there wasn't a train she could catch.

Or was there?

There was a bewildering number of folders to sort through. Kris didn't know exactly what she was looking for. She opened one folder and found a list of every agent working for Toor. Another held schematics for the base. One of the folders had a grocery list: *Eggs. Milk. Bread...*

A fourth folder entitled Code Red almost made Kris fall off her chair. It contained one short message marked with today's date:

Third orb in Beijing*. City evacuated, no civilian losses.*

Kris covered her mouth with her hands. The orbs kept coming, and there was nothing she or anyone could do to stop them.

She remembered when they'd first arrived on the base. She could see it clearly in her mind. There had been supply trucks. One of the soldiers had been talking about taking supplies to the "alpha base."

That name, "alpha base," seemed important. Was it a fuel depot? A food storage facility?

Or was it where the orb was?

Kris reopened the base schematics. She couldn't find anything about the alpha base, but she studied the layout and memorized a secure route to get to the supply trucks. Easy enough—she'd stow away on one that was heading to New York City. She'd have to be in the right place at the exact right time and avoid detection, which meant leaving in the middle of the night. But in theory, it could work.

Once Kris got to Times Square, she'd visit the orb. Then she could ask one of the guards for help; they could bring her back to the base. That is, if they didn't shoot her first. The whole thing was too absurd. It was best not to think about the details of getting back. The main thing now was getting to the orb. She could worry about what came next later.

Kris returned to her dream and its vivid images, that voice. It was the strangest thing she'd ever heard—it was like many voices talking at once, like a chorus backed by a swelling orchestra of thousands. And the music had been there too.

Kris jolted. She was late for the eight-thirty M-Team meeting. Nate would be pissed, like the time she'd been late for their first meeting at the university. His annoyed stare in that big office filled with all those books had made her feel so small.

"He's a genius, though," she mumbled. A genius among geniuses. And he was protecting her now.

Kris wasn't sure he had ever approved of her. He was hot, then cold. Working on her doctorate with him had often felt like a surreal game of "who's the better mathematician." He'd taken any chance to test her, like the time he'd ridiculed her in front of other students during her seminar talk on the Collatz conjecture. She'd shrunk in front of the audience of late twentysomethings while he looked on with smug disapproval.

Good wasn't good enough for him. He'd always expected her to be the best.

She'd taken the challenge and persevered. She'd been able to do mathematics that Nate's other students couldn't, and they'd resented her for it. They'd shot her cold glances, treated her as if she were an alien. They'd never even asked her to join them for coffee. Not once.

The orb's flashing message played in slow motion on her screen, the solitary light in her otherwise dark space. It was hypnotic, and she knew there was a meaning to the pattern. It wasn't random noise. The message had structure.

If she closed her eyes, she could hear the music of the orb. The sound wrapped heavily around her.

Kris ran into the workroom so fast she tripped over a stack of books that fell with a dull thud. Lara chuckled, all low and raspy. She was the oldest on the M-Team and one of Kris's idols. There were a dozen mathematicians, living and dead, whom she loved and wanted to be more like—icons like Katherine Johnson, Emmy Noether, and Paul Erdős. Lara Armistead, who worked in infinite-dimensional geometry, was one of the more recent ones. Her wrinkled forehead was partially covered with silver bangs. She looked like an older version of Antoinette if she were French. She was so cool. Parisian cool.

Nate didn't look impressed as Kris grabbed the scattered books.

Like the sleeping quarters, the workroom was also stark white with no windows, but it contained five white tables and chairs, framed by giant boards that doubled as large screens. The black cups of steaming coffee stood out starkly against the white walls and furnishings. Nate sat waiting; he hated to wait.

"Dr. Argentia, how good of you to grace us with your presence," he said in his best sarcastic professor tone. Kris didn't respond, staring at the screens filled with the M-Team's morning work.

"You'll be happy to know that while you were *sleeping*, we had a breakthrough in the second part of the message. Using ideas from four-manifolds, we found a useful algorithm for segmenting the alien message. See block seventy-seven H on the left middle screen—"

"I'd double-check that part if I were you. Did you get my email?" Kris said, interrupting him.

The members of the M-Team turned to look at her. "I read it but didn't understand it," Benedita said. Lara and Luke said nothing.

Kris blinked and fidgeted with her index finger and thumb. She'd done something wrong again. Another faux pas? She wished she could make him happy for once.

"Kris, what are you talking about?" Nate said.

"The derivation is wrong. The error is in the second screen on the right, eleventh line…block forty-three E."

Nate turned a paler color as he reviewed the proof, then changed hue once again. He saw the mistake now.

"*Puta merda!*" he said. He resorted to Brazilian swear words when he was angry or excited. Kris had met his mother last year, who'd taken him on a summer trip as a child to her native Rio de Janeiro.

Lara lit a cigarette.

Nate waved his hands in front of his face. "Do you have to light that in here? If the orbs don't all kill us, the secondhand smoke will," he said.

She took one slow drag, studying him. "*Voyons.* Everyone here is always afraid of the wrong things," she said. "But if it reassures you..."

She dropped the cigarette into her half-full coffee cup and let it drown.

"Let me show you something," Kris said. "Here's what I discovered last night about the message."

Nate said nothing as Kris uploaded her work to the screens, displacing the work of the team. "I had the idea to apply Ramsey theory to the message to break each segment into even smaller parts. Maybe that'll help us solve it."

The room shifted for Kris as the upload completed. Not physically, but the way the air tightens before a storm, when even the birds fall silent. The patterns stabilized at once. She leaned closer, her pulse ticking in her ears. Raw data didn't do this. The message wasn't revealing itself so much as allowing itself to be seen, and she couldn't look away.

Several pages of formulas and three-dimensional plots of the message popped up on one of the large screens, visible to all. Kris described how the message was a nonlinear, high-dimensional code with at least ten mirror symmetries.

"I'll work on the symmetries. I can run one of my deciphering algorithms to map them out," Luke said. He was a big shot in number theory from MIT, a middle-aged guy with broad shoulders, a plaid shirt, and a longish brown beard. He had a smooth, dark complexion, brown beard, and red hair pulled back in a tight bun. Luke began to write formulas on a screen.

The rest of the M-Team buzzed as they set about analyzing this new approach. Nate shot Kris a glare, and she knew that despite her breakthrough, he wasn't happy.

"Kris, a word outside. Now," Nate said. His normal color had returned, but his face was grim. They walked out into the hall, and he closed the door.

"You look terrible. Did you sleep?"

"Not much. I was up most of the night."

"Do you know the story of how I came to be your supervisor?"

"Yeah. The chair was trying to find someone to work with me, and you made sense because of your number theory and combinatorics stuff. You're super picky taking new students, and you didn't really want to, but you still said yes."

"Wrong. I asked to work with you. I've followed your career since you were twelve. I never imagined someone your age could do what you can. You're the most gifted mathematician I've ever met. You'll stand alongside Ramanujan, Turing, and Emmy Noether. You'll win a Fields Medal."

"I don't care about that," Kris said, crossing her arms.

"You say that now," Nate replied. "One day, you'll understand why recognition of your work matters. But claiming you can prove the Riemann hypothesis is something else entirely. That's like claiming you've found a cure for cancer, so excuse me if I'm skeptical."

He didn't wait for her response. "You are not to tell the rest of the M-Team. Not until I've checked the details. That could take weeks. It could take months. It may never happen at all, especially given the current crisis."

Kris blushed. Why was he telling her this now?

"And right now, you're acting like a spoiled child," he added with a sour expression.

Kris's mouth opened in shock. That was like a slap in the face.

"Excuse me? I'm not a child!" Kris's hands shook with anger. He'd never talked to her like that before.

"Then act like a grown-up. You've always presented yourself as an adult in a kid's body. You can do mathematics that most of us can't, but being an adult comes with responsibility. You can't sleep in and miss M-Team meetings. I appreciate the breakthrough and your sharing it with us. But you're not in charge. We need to work together seriously on this, especially since the stakes are so high."

Her cheeks were hot. She could feel the anger seething inside her. Maybe Antoinette's Dr. Asshole assessment was right after all.

"I do...I do take it seriously. How dare you?" she said, her voice quivering. "Sarah is gone," Kris continued in a half whisper.

Nate's face softened. "I know that. Sarah is my friend, and I want her back too. I need you here, working *with* the team. Together, we have the best chance of solving this and getting her back."

Kris remained quiet and blinked back a tear in her right eye.

"And by the way, did it even occur to you that the four-manifold approach could provide an alternative parsing algorithm?"

Kris wiped her eye. Nate was a gigantic mathematical talent, but he could be a jerk.

"I hadn't considered that," she muttered.

"No, you hadn't. If you hadn't walked into the workroom with such an attitude, then you might have appreciated our approach, even if there was a *minor* error."

He coughed. He choked on the word.

Nate paced as he made his next point, pleading. "This isn't a competition. We're at *war*. Do you understand? The aliens have taken millions of our people, and more orbs are popping up as we speak. There's a third one now, in Beijing."

Kris lifted her hands to her mouth. She hoped it looked like a surprise.

"The story gets better. As the President told me in our scientific update meeting this morning, China has sealed its borders and is on high nuclear alert. There's intensified fighting at the Pakistan–India border, and the Palestinians and Israelis are lobbing missiles at each other. This is a disaster on a global scale, potentially worse than any pandemic or world war."

Kris knew he was telling the truth; his hands were shaking as he spoke. "It's okay. We'll work as a team on the message and make progress," she offered.

"We may not be fast enough. Either the aliens will make us all vanish, or we'll blow each other up. Typical stupid, reactionary measures from undeveloped bipedal primates who evolved out of living in trees."

"Do you remember the day I told you about my proof of the Collatz conjecture?" Kris asked.

"Like it was yesterday. You disappeared for a month and wouldn't take my calls. Then you ran into my office, spilling coffee all over my desk."

"Other mathematicians said it was impossible. But I did it," Kris said. Kris remembered the day: coffee everywhere, Nate half laughing, half furious, and amazed.

"You did. You made the impossible possible. I said that after I read your proof. We must do it again—do the impossible to solve the message." His eyes hardened. "We need to get back to the workroom. Let's merge our two approaches. Sound okay?" he asked.

Kris's stomach ached and her temples throbbed. She was hungry and yearned for a hot cup of coffee. And she had to tell Antoinette about her plans to go to New York City.

Everything depended on her making contact with the orb.

Ari sat alone again in the mess hall, an empty plate in front of him. Why didn't Toor ever eat with him?

Seeing him made Kris feel lighter, distracted her from the unforgiving toil of the M-Team. He was the one other teen on the base besides Antoinette. She'd wandered off to escape the workroom, which was like a pressure cooker. Even a few minutes away helped. Nate had given her a stern look when she'd left, as if she had to complete a sign-out sheet to go pee. She knew she couldn't stay away too long or he'd call her out again, and that would make her head explode.

"Come here often?" she said, sitting next to him.

He shot her a toothy grin. His whole face lit up when he smiled. "I met Antoinette this morning at breakfast. She's cool."

"That's her, all right. My cool big sister. I'm taking a mini-break from the M-Team right now."

"Mom said you guys are hard at work. All heavy-duty math

problems. I'd like to join you guys, but I don't have a PhD. Instead I'm sleeping in, listening to music, reading math books, and playing chess with some soldier called Private Dax."

Kris shrugged. "Mathematical talent isn't about degrees. It's about intuition and creativity and hard work. Or at least that's what Nate—er, Dr. Wallace says." She was on the verge of babbling, so she quit talking.

Ari's face hardened. A lock of hair fell over his forehead, and he pushed it back. His eyes reminded her of Toor's, dark and tough like black diamonds. Kris looked down at her fingernails. They needed clipping. A few moments passed in silence.

"So...can I tell you something?" Ari asked, his voice hushed. "You have to promise not to say anything to anyone."

Kris looked up. His gaze was roaming the room. A handful of soldiers in green fatigues were eating in the corner about twenty feet away, and one worker was behind the counter, wiping down trays. Otherwise, the cafeteria was empty. A beam of yellow sunlight poured through one of the windows at the top of the wall opposite them. There were so few windows in the base; Kris welcomed the trickle of light.

She bit her lip and he moved closer to her.

"I'm having this weird recurring dream...about the aliens."

She leaned forward even more to listen. She could feel Ari's warm breath in her ear now.

"In the dream, I'm in a field, one that goes on forever in all directions. It's covered in grass. There's a blue sky with fluffy white clouds. Floating above me is an orb."

Kris pulled back and met his gaze. There was fear there.

"And it calls me something. A single word. It's so absurd—it must be a nightmare."

Kris gasped. "*Maker*," she said.

His eyes betrayed his surprise. "You've had them too," he said.

She swallowed hard; her mouth was parched. "How long have you had these dreams?" she asked.

"Since the night the orbs came. I told Mom, but she said nothing. There's a link between the orbs and me. The dreams feel so, so real."

"I had a dream like that last night." Kris could see the orb flashing in her mind's eye and heard those voices.

Ari stared at her for a long time, saying nothing. Then he asked, "If you have more dreams like that, Doc Kris, would you please let me know?"

His pen rolled off the table, and they both tried to pick it up, their fingers touching for an instant. They locked stares for a second, and Kris let out an involuntary giggle.

As she walked back to the workroom, she thought, *He's having the dreams too*. Her brain was going into hyperdrive. Her dreams were not random. Maybe there were others having them too, besides her and Ari. The orbs were trying to speak with them through dreams, and Kris had no clue why. Why couldn't the aliens send an email or a text or flash a video on a screen?

The dreams weren't meant for her alone.

The afternoon flew by for Kris as the M-Team worked on their theories. The team was free to eat, rest, and break off into smaller groups as they desired. Kris had worked alone for the most part, though she'd talked to Benedita about the technical details of her approach. Kris found the woman to be the most approachable; maybe it was her age. When Kris had gotten into a mathematical debate with Luke earlier in the day, he'd shut her down by pointing out how young she was. Nate had intervened, but Kris was used to this kind of reaction from other mathematicians. She didn't feel her age—at least, not when working.

With the next formal meeting set to convene tomorrow after breakfast at eight a.m., Kris took a breather. The evening was fresh, and Venus shone on the horizon. She wandered along a pathway encircling the base, kicking up dust. The chain-link and barbed wire fence that ran alongside her hammered home where she was.

She wished she were back at home. She spent most of her time there working on mathematics too, but it was safe. Comfortable. It would have been so much easier if she'd been there now, at her desk, bent over the problem.

Kris found her way to Antoinette, who was strumming her guitar on the bed. The sight of her alone in the sterile white quarters made Kris uneasy. They were so far from home and what they knew.

"Hey there, K. Did you save the world yet?"

"Hmmm." She exhaled and fell onto Antoinette's bed, leaving the door open an inch. The wool blanket scratched her legs.

Antoinette pulled at Kris's ponytail, and her blond hair fell around her shoulders. "Sounds bad."

"They were working on smooth four-manifolds, but I told them it was wrong. Then I explained my ideas using Ramsey theory. From there, we resolved a segment of the message by exploiting mirror symmetries in the four-manifold using quantum algorithms..."

Antoinette narrowed her eyes. Kris could tell she was going into way too much detail. Antoinette had still been a little kid when she'd encountered the freaky, unreal world of mathematical brilliance. Kris had received most of Sarah's attention. Being around mathematicians was a constant in Antoinette's life too, though, whether she liked it or not. Antoinette had heard words like "perfectoids" and "concentration inequalities" and "logarithmic density" for years as Kris had chatted with Nate over Rix. She knew more math than she let on. And she knew what the process of mathematical discovery was like, having watched Kris stay up late and get up early while wrestling with her latest problem. Her eyes glazed over, though, whenever Kris attempted to explain her latest mathematical conquest.

"You heard about China? The orb appeared in Beijing to a whopping audience of nobody," Antoinette said, changing the subject. She projected a screen on the wall showing riots in London. "The king left for an island or something."

"What have you been up to?" Kris asked.

"I'm writing a new song. I figured that when we get the other members of The Nettes back or whatever, maybe we can land a contract with a major record label."

The first time Kris had heard The Nettes play was four years ago, the day after the world-famous Dr. Nathaniel Wallace had agreed to supervise her doctoral thesis. That day was Kris's best memory from being twelve.

Paula's voice was clear and beautiful. Antoinette was a natural on guitar—what she lacked in technique, she made up for in raw fearlessness. She was self-taught, staying up all night watching and rewatching online lessons on Rix. Sarah had always encouraged her music, even offering to pay for lessons with a real live instructor.

"What's your song called?" Kris asked.

"It doesn't have a title yet. I'll play it."

Kris sat up and leaned against the wall, which was cold against her back. Antoinette began strumming the guitar and singing in her half-spoken, husky singing voice. The song was all bouncy dream-pop but also with dark undertones like a brewing thunderstorm.

There's nothing but the stars,
there's nothing but the sea,
there's nothing but the moon and sun and you.

It's all about the tears,
it's all about the loss,
it's all about the earth and sky and you.

The sun. The moon. And you.
The stars. The sea. And you.
The sun. The moon. And you. In you.

I'm altogether gone,
I'm altogether lost,
I'm altogether gone and lost in you.

So happy when you're here,
so sad when you're gone.
Nothing feels the same when I'm with you.

The song stirred Kris's memories like a stick poking a hornet's nest. Her mom. Her home, with its rows of black-eyed Susans in the front garden, their tiny lawn anchored by a single crab apple tree. A week ago, she'd wanted to escape that place with every fiber of her being. She planned on getting her license and driving across Canada, traveling from Toronto along the Trans-Canada Highway all the way to Fogo Island in Newfoundland. There, she could lazily watch whales and icebergs while sipping a Coke. Or hop on a plane to Paris and visit the Louvre and the Eiffel Tower and eat crème brûlée in a sidewalk café while it rained.

Her mom was uncool—she nagged Kris about staying up late doing mathematics and about the millions of scattered papers everywhere. But Kris would have given her soul to be back in that bungalow, to hug Sarah tight and never let go. Tucked away in her memory, home was out of reach and hundreds of miles away. Sarah was light years away and possibly gone forever.

As Antoinette's song finished, Kris's chest tightened as if the air inside had disappeared.

"I love it," Kris said. When Antoinette played, she always imagined the invisible harmonies she heard in her mind while doing math.

"You think you're the only one with mad talents?"

Now, Antoinette was all she had left, and she needed her sister's support. Kris took her hand, squeezing it hard until her knuckles went white. She had to tell her. She could trust her.

"I'm going to Times Square."

"What the hell? With the M-Team?" Antoinette's face contorted, and she let Kris's hand go.

"Nah. They aren't coming, and I need you to keep this a secret, at least until I come back," Kris whispered. If Antoinette told Nate, her plan to visit the orb would be over before it began. They hated each other, but Kris was worried, nevertheless.

"Do you have a death wish? No way. Why?"

"The orbs are calling me. I've been having these dreams... It's hard to explain, but I have to go. I think...I think we can get Mom back if I speak to an orb in the right way."

Kris explained the dreams, and Antoinette's eyes widened each time she mentioned Sarah. The dreams were more than a coincidence, Kris explained. She knew she could hear and talk to the aliens. She'd done it in the moments before the flash at Sankofa Square, and now in her dreams. They called her "Maker."

Antoinette paused, her face hardening. She looked fierce with her dark eyeliner and black hair. "Then I'm coming too."

Kris shook her head. "No way. It's too dangerous. I can't ask you to come. If they catch you, they'll send you to a camp. And if anything happened to you...I couldn't live with myself."

Antoinette's face softened, and Kris took her hand again.

"Okay. You're officially bananas," Antoinette said. "You'll need me. I'm the reckless one."

Kris hugged her, relieved that she wouldn't have to do this alone.

"I'm going to stow away on a supply truck. There's one leaving at midnight, and I know a way we can get on it without getting caught." Kris's heart pumped hard from the adrenaline. If her sister ratted her out, it was all over.

"Remind me to bring you along when I rob a bank." Antoinette put her hand to her mouth and chewed on the nail of her right index finger.

"Please promise you won't tell anyone, especially not Nate or Toor."

Antoinette's face contorted. "Give me a break, K. Dr. Asshole is the last person I would trust. And Madam CIA is a hard pass."

"Can you do one more thing for me?"

"Anything."

Kris paused like she was going to spill a big secret. Antoinette went still.

"Paint my nails black?"

Antoinette laughed under her breath.

"'Nothing but the Stars' is the title of your song. That'll make you a million bucks for sure," Kris said.

After a late dinner in the mess hall, Kris said good night to the M-Team. She walked the short path to her room, the corridor stretching ahead of her, her footsteps steady while the rest of the base receded. Ten p.m. She couldn't relax. Her skin felt like it was crawling with ants, and anxiety churned in her stomach.

She detoured to the meeting room and stood by the open door. Lara and Benedita were talking at a screen. No one noticed her there. She watched them in silence as they exchanged ideas—they were making steady progress. They had deciphered another few bits of the message, in large part owing to her breakthrough the night before.

Nate was his usual self. He had called her a spoiled child. Next, he might ridicule her in public as he'd done those long months ago during her doctoral seminar. That embarrassed feeling gripped her and wouldn't let go, squeezing in from all sides. The dreams she'd experienced the night before intruded into her mind. The orb was calling to her. She *had* to see it with her own eyes. That way, she could talk to the aliens and get Mom back.

Kris ran through the mental image in her mind of the schematics she'd pulled up about the military base. Her black fingernails glared back at her like angry crows. The next supply truck would depart just after midnight.

A new Kris emerged. *They want a misfit, so I'll give them one*, she thought.

Kris packed a small bag, then knocked gently on Antoinette's door. It was time to execute their plan.

CHAPTER 6

NEXUS

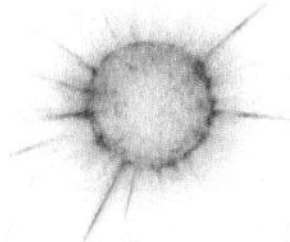

"**R**EADY, K?" ANTOINETTE asked.

"Five by five," Kris said, curling her black nails into her fists.

Getting into the back of the supply truck was the easy bit. It was just after midnight on Thursday morning, and the base was quiet. At this hour, the soldiers were tired and less attentive than usual. Kris and Antoinette had snuck away while the others were sleeping. They'd stuffed Kris's backpack with the essentials: water, phones, snacks, flashlights, and Kris's diary. Antoinette scraped her knee getting in the truck and cursed under her breath.

Security was low at night; only a few guards were stationed around the base. The military kept only a skeleton crew in the city too—the massive wave of refugees in the camps took most of their effort and resources. According to the files Kris had read, New York had only a small crew of soldiers stationed at the bridges and checkpoints. They'd evacuated Manhattan and the surrounding boroughs, and the whole area was now under martial law.

But Kris needed to see the orb in person rather than on a two-dimensional screen. She knew with every cell of her body that it wanted her to come to Times Square. Antoinette agreed that communicating with it was the best way to get Sarah back. Could she also bring back the millions of other vanished people?

What she was doing was reckless and stupid, but it was a plan.

Huddled with her sister in the back of the truck, there it was again: that nagging sense of not belonging. Kris closed her eyes, letting the chaos run its course until patterns began to surface. She didn't like the labels of "math genius" or "prodigy." They made her feel distant from other people. That was why she couldn't relate to the M-Team. A day and a half of work had felt like weeks. Nate had called her a child, and Luke had done the same.

She didn't feel like a child, though she did feel like an orphan.

Kris was used to working alone, chatting with Nate for validation and support. But this was so different from anything she had done before. The M-Team didn't seem to get her. She did her best work alone. Nate treated them like a glorified group of graduate students jumping through his imaginary hoops. But Kris knew better. She knew that the way to solving the message wasn't in linear steps but in big intuitive leaps. And how could she go wrong with her big sis by her side?

"Are you sleeping?" Antoinette whispered.

Kris opened her eyes and could just make out the silhouette of her sister's face in the darkness of the truck. She took a few deep breaths. There was a fresh smell like rain and antiseptic.

"No. Thinking. Sleeping and thinking can look the same," Kris responded.

Kris wiped sweat from her brow. Even inside the truck, she could feel the summer heat radiating from the concrete walkways in the depot. If they were lucky, she and Antoinette could get to Times Square and rescue everybody or at least get some information. If they weren't, Toor would likely send her and Antoinette to a relocation camp.

Kris snapped back to reality as voices sounded near the truck. She heard the dull thud of the truck door, and the vehicle moved. Loaded with food and other supplies, it was scheduled to restock various checkpoints throughout the city, providing essentials for the next few days to the soldiers patrolling the vacant streets. Being one of the few souls left in the ghost city must have been a quiet, unsettling experience.

Among the tied-down boxes, Kris and Antoinette fidgeted, trying to get comfortable. One of the nearby crates was loose. Antoinette lifted the top and peered in with the small flashlight she'd picked up at the base. She pulled out a sealed bag containing a sandwich and held it up to Kris with a questioning look. Peanut butter—that would do nicely. Antoinette stocked her knapsack with sandwiches.

"You doing okay over there?" Antoinette whispered.

Kris lit her flashlight under her chin and said, "Boo."

The truck jostled, making Kris nauseated. She breathed deeply, and it passed. She wanted to rest and closed her eyes again.

The pull of the orb was impossible for Kris to resist. She *had* to do this—it was as if she were under its spell. Toor would think she lost it and confine her to her room. But Kris had to see the orb for herself, maybe even touch its surface.

The orb had called her "Maker." The maker of what? What did the orbs want from her? They had called to Ari too. Maybe she should have asked him to come.

The monotonous, soft drone of the electric engines and the near darkness made Kris drowsy. A large bump in the road shifted the loose crate she was leaning against, and the feeling passed.

The truck stopped briefly at what was likely a checkpoint and then drove into the heart of the city. Kris couldn't see anything. Aside from the engine and the shuffling of the crates, it was quiet. Too quiet for a big city like New York.

The truck stopped, and the driver got out. Kris heard the murmur of conversation and smelled exhaust in the air. Antoinette put a finger to her mouth, her eyes darting around. Soon the voices faded, and silence returned.

Antoinette cracked open the solid rear door and leaned out. They were on another military base, this one much smaller than the one housing the M-Team. No one was there, so they jumped out. Kris's backpack was heavy, full of sandwiches she'd taken from the crate and bottles of water from the mess hall. The base was deserted, but she knew that it wasn't. The exit was about thirty feet to her left. Antoinette looked around, and then they began a slow jog, turning their heads from side to side.

To Kris's amazement, no one called out to them. She'd imagined that one of the soldiers would catch her. She turned her phone on for a few seconds and got reception, then lost it again. The cell network must've been working, however badly.

"Turn that thing off, you dork," Antoinette said in a sharp whisper. Kris turned it off. Antoinette was right. Someone could track it.

She strained her neck, looking up at the tall buildings as they headed down the deserted street; all of them were dark. The moon was half full, the sky clear, and her eyes adjusted to the dim light. Broadway and 42nd was where they needed to go. Antoinette had visited Manhattan with her bandmates during her last year of high school. Mom had been furious when she'd come home with a black eye after getting into a fight at a nightclub, but now Kris was glad that at least one of them had a passing familiarity with the city.

Kris shuddered as she walked with her sister through the empty streets of the city. Newspapers and litter were scattered on the ground. Smashed yellow taxis and countless cars lined the sides of the roads, though most of the streets were clear of vehicles. Either the cars had gotten out of downtown before the orb had struck or the military had removed them. Maybe some of each.

Despite the warmth of the summer night, Kris was cold. She felt small, walking through the corridors of dark skyscrapers.

Someone yelled, and they ducked into a doorway, hiding as best they could. A rush of panic struck her, and her hands trembled. She didn't want to think about what else might be out there, soldiers or otherwise.

Kris waited a few minutes before moving forward again, gripping the small flashlight in her pocket. She and Antoinette were alone in this place, defenseless if their plans went south. Her hands trembled.

More time passed in silence. Antoinette sat down on a stoop and pulled out a pair of sleek wireless earbuds.

"You still carry those around?" Kris asked.

"Don't judge me." She popped one into her ear and handed Kris the other.

Music spilled in, the bass heavy, loud enough to make Kris blink. Antoinette was already swaying, snapping her fingers. She tugged Kris's hand, so she bobbed her head like she'd seen her sister do at concerts. She felt ridiculous, stiff as ever.

Antoinette laughed. "You're such a mega geek. But at least you're trying. The black nails help."

They were just two sisters, not a prodigy and her keeper.

"Can I ask you something serious?" Kris said.

"Sure, shoot," Antoinette replied.

"Other than Mom, what do you miss most? You know, from before all this wildness happened?"

"I miss staying up late with friends," Antoinette said, wincing. Kris put her arm around her.

Antoinette cleared her throat, and her eyelids fluttered. "We were going to go to Berlin in October. Paula has a super cool buddy, Ina, who said she'd let us crash at her apartment. We were going to visit David Bowie's old flat in Neukölln, maybe even busk outside it. It's a café now."

"I miss home-cooked meals," Kris responded.

"I miss playing my songs at full blast when you and Sarah are out."

"I miss Terence Tao's math notes on Rix."

"What the…?" Antoinette choked on her laughter. Her reaction puzzled Kris, but she grinned. A mosquito whined around Kris's ear and landed on her hand. She swatted at it, and it flew away.

"Do you ever wish you were more like me?" Kris asked.

"The thing is, sis, you aren't the center of the universe. I've got my own gig. But sure, sometimes I imagine what it would be like to have a PhD at sixteen. To be a freak of nature."

Kris was silent. She did feel like a freak at least once a day. She'd been homeschooled as a kid and had never attended high school. She longed to be one of the normie kids sometimes, but even on a good day, fitting in was a challenge.

"I wish I could be more like you," Kris said.

"Don't get weird on me."

"You're tough, and you always know what to do." Kris put her head on Antoinette's shoulder. For once, Antoinette let her.

"I've got something new to show you. Point the flashlight here," Antoinette said, pulling her black hair back to reveal a small skull image behind her right ear. The skin around the fresh tattoo was pink.

"No way! When did you get that? Mom will kill you." Needles scared Kris, and she had no desire to get inked.

"I was going to show you on Monday, but then everything went haywire. Doesn't it look killer? I almost put it on my boob but chickened out."

Kris chuckled.

Antoinette's face turned serious. "We've got a mission. Let's go."

New York reminded Kris of Toronto, but larger and more dense. She had memorized the route to Times Square from the northeast. The city was laid out in a logical grid, the numbers descending as they went south. Times Square was between 42nd and 47th. She laughed to herself. Most people's first visit involved a Broadway show, not stowing away in a military cargo truck. She had definitely broken the recommended order of operations.

◎ ◦ ◎

Kris crouched next to her sister and tried hard not to make a sound.

"Be extra quiet," Antoinette said, her lips barely moving.

Kris's heart pounded so hard she imagined she could hear it beating like a drum outside her body. There was a sound of breaking glass to their right, along with two deep male voices. She and Antoinette crouched on a staircase leading to the black basement door of a building with red-painted bricks. Kris didn't dare to look over the ledge that was hiding her and Antoinette from the owners of those voices.

She had caught a brief glance at the pair of men before ducking for cover. The taller of the two wore a brown leather jacket and a black toque, and the other wore a black hoodie and tan construction boots. As far as Kris could tell, they were breaking into a restaurant. She strained to hear their words but could only hear Antoinette's short breaths beside her.

In the three days that had passed since the incident with the orb at Times Square, the city had been fully evacuated, save for the military presence. But the soldiers and helicopters couldn't be everywhere. Kris imagined civilians sneaking around the city. They could've been looking for their loved ones or—more likely—breaking into the vast metropolis to steal what they could.

Like money or jewelry meant anything now.

The orb had taken everyone who'd been unable to evacuate, exactly like what had happened in Sankofa Square. The bridges into the city were guarded, so the pair must have found some other way to get into Manhattan. They were breaking into a restaurant, not a bank, so maybe they were hungry, not greedy. The latter made much more sense to Kris than the former, but she couldn't be sure of their motives.

Manhattan wasn't impregnable. After all, they'd gotten in.

"What do we do?" Kris whispered as softly as she could.

"Dunno. Wait for them to piss off and hope they don't see us?"

Kris calculated several strategies to evade the men if they were discovered. Unfortunately, she didn't feel confident that any of them would succeed.

"Hey," hissed a voice.

Kris froze. The voice had come from her left, in the opposite direction of the looters. She heard footsteps on the broken glass near the restaurant and loud but unintelligible chatter.

Antoinette lifted her head over the ledge and then ducked again. She smirked, and Kris's stomach sank.

"You'll never believe it. It's *Ari*," Antoinette said with fire in her eyes.

Kris bit her fingernail on her left thumb. How had he gotten here?

"Come quick!" Ari said in a whisper-shout.

Kris locked eyes with Antoinette, then headed up the stairs, being careful not to trip. She glanced over at the shattered door of the restaurant. Darkness. No one was there.

She ran, followed by Antoinette. Ari raced ahead, running southward down the wide, dark street. As she turned a corner, Kris grazed her shoulder on a brick wall and almost tripped. She winced in pain.

They followed Ari two blocks south and turned right onto a narrow side street. Ari passed through the open glass door of a hair salon. Kris shuffled in with Antoinette in tow. Her shoulder hurt, but the tingling pain of the scrape began to subside. In the inky darkness, Ari pointed to a back door and opened it with a creak.

Kris paused to listen for the voices of the looters, but they were only faint echoes in her memory. There was silence. She steadied herself and walked through the door.

"What the hell are you doing here?" Antoinette said, her eyes all menacing.

Shadows danced on Ari's face as he fumbled with a flashlight app on his phone, and it dimly illuminated the space. They crouched on the floor of the salon's storage room, full of boxes and shelves holding beauty supplies. Kris made out a paper heart tacked to the wall on her right with A LOVES D 2001 scrawled in curly letters.

Ari smelled of sweat, and he took rapid breaths. There was a short pause. He stared at Kris, wide-eyed.

"I'm here to see the orb, like you and Doc Kris."

Kris cleared her throat. Her chest still burned from the run through the dark streets. Antoinette stared at Ari defiantly and crossed her arms.

"I heard you two talking about coming here. I wasn't spying. I swear. I was bored and came by to chat. That was when I heard Kris's plan." Kris remembered leaving Antoinette's door open an inch.

"You could have told us that you wanted to come with us," Kris said.

"That would've been too dangerous. Mom—I mean, Agent Toor could have found out. I gambled and came alone. It's not the first time I've run away."

"How did you get here? Did Toor send you?" asked Antoinette.

He let out a sigh. "No, I came on my own. Another truck left a few minutes after yours. I saw you stow away in the first one, then I did the same in the second. I followed you until you ducked away from the looters," he said. He grinned with pride.

"Why risk your life to come here? It's too weird," Antoinette said, leaning back against the wall and wiping her face with her hand.

"No, it makes perfect sense," Kris said. "He's been having the same dreams as me. The orbs drew him in too."

Antoinette's eyes narrowed. "When were you going to tell me that?"

"Whatever, now he's here, and it's done," Kris responded.

"I suppose we should thank you for your help with those looting goons. But understand something, Dumbo Ears. You ain't the main attraction here—Kris is. She needs to get close to the orb and try to communicate with it. She's the priority."

Ari scowled. Kris didn't think he liked the nickname Antoinette had given him.

"Let's rest here for a few minutes and make sure we are alone. The looters could have seen us and followed us. Then we're going to find the orb, unless we're murdered by soldiers," Antoinette said.

Kris met Ari's gaze, and his face settled into a no-holds-barred smile.

Dawn would come in a few hours.

Times Square wasn't what Kris had expected. At least, it wasn't like what she'd seen on-screen. The skyscrapers on all sides were dark and empty, and the bustle of tourists, vendors, cars, and street performers was gone. All the tall screens were dark now, looming like ominous black holes. No one was there. At least, no humans.

At the corner of 42nd and Broadway was the orb, all alone.

Antoinette jumped. The orb flashed its messages to an absent audience. Kris felt a tugging sensation deep in her chest, as if the street sloped downward toward the orb. She swallowed hard and stopped resisting the pull.

"You sure this is smart?" Antoinette said.

"No, probably not," Kris said.

"We have to be here," Ari said.

"It's unbelievable. A real live alien *thing* is floating right there," Antoinette said.

"I've got to get closer," Kris said.

"Wait for me."

They moved straight toward it, and an odd sensation began in Kris's temples, as if she were waking up from a dream or trudging through snow that grew deeper as she moved. They walked toward the alien artifact, three figures accompanied by their moonlit shadows. Her heart pounded, and her stomach churned with excitement.

"Do you know what you're going to do?" Antoinette asked.

"No. There's no instruction manual for this. I'm not sure why I'm even here or what I expect to see."

"What if the thing goes all glowy and vaporizes us?"

"I don't think it will. I'll try to be careful."

Kris took a deep breath. Her ears were so hot that they itched.

"Wait. Lemme try to communicate with it first," Ari said. His eyes darted around, taking in the patterns on the orb.

"Absolutely friggin' not! That's not the deal. We came here to bring *Kris* to the orb, not you."

"But I'm having the dreams too—"

Antoinette shook her head. "Can you believe this jerk?" she said, cutting him off mid-sentence. Ari raised his finger to his mouth as if to silence her with a magic spell.

That was when the world changed.

Kris suddenly felt as if she were moving in slow motion, like she was underwater. Antoinette froze like a marble statue, as did the street around them. Kris moved her hand back and forth in front of her face, and it left fading trails of light.

Ari walked toward the orb, which was now glowing like the sun. The mathematical message streamed over its surface, brighter and more powerful than before. Kris gasped at the infinite maze of self-replicating patterns.

She closed her eyes. Even at a distance, she could see the white flashes of the orb through her eyelids. There were voices in her head, all garbled and mumbling. And they were growing louder.

Ari walked toward the orb, the only thing moving in a world of marble statues. He could stop time! He ran ahead of Kris and Antoinette. Standing close to the orb, he placed both his palms on its surface. Ari's hands glowed. Kris grew hotter, as if she were on fire.

The voices came into painful focus inside Kris's head. "Not the Maker," they bellowed.

Ari flew backward as if pushed by a powerful gust of wind, landing on his side beside Kris. The orb turned bright red, then black. The patterns began to flash once more. Ari opened his eyes, and his face contorted in pain.

The world began to move again. Antoinette hadn't seen him approach the orb.

"He thinks he is in charge here," she continued. "Wait, why is he lying on the ground?"

"You okay?" Kris asked Ari. He didn't answer. He looked at her, swallowed, and his jaw tightened. She shuddered as it was her turn. She walked forward, and Antoinette followed. Ari sat on the ground with his head bowed and cradled the shoulder he'd fallen on.

Standing a few dozen feet away from the orb, Kris closed her eyes. She could see the white lights of the message through her closed lids. The symbols created a kind of kaleidoscope. The patterns and their hidden message were bewildering. Antoinette squeezed her hand, providing an anchor to reality.

Images flickered through her mind, a garbled torrent of nonsensical symbols. Kris strained to make sense of the pattern but couldn't. It was moving too fast, and she couldn't see any structure in the chaos.

She walked closer until she was standing inches from the orb. She had a giddy feeling like vertigo. Her eyelids flickered before the dazzling light show.

"Don't touch it!" Ari shouted.

Kris looked over her shoulder. Antoinette was shaking her head. "Yeah, it's too dangerous," she said.

"I've got to make contact. We can find out where Mom is," Kris said with a dry mouth. She turned back to the orb. "Maker is here. Now tell me what that means."

Her trembling hand touched the orb, and there was a pulse. Time stopped, like when she'd seen Sarah freeze in Sankofa Square. Antoinette froze too, not blinking, not breathing.

Kris heard music, soft at first, then growing louder. The surface of the orb sparkled with jewels. That was when the lights went out.

Kris looked around, bleary-eyed. The streets were empty. Antoinette and Ari were gone! Kris's heart pounded, and her eyes darted around, looking for her sister. Her breath came in gasps as she ran around the area.

"Ant? Where are you?" She fought back tears. She was alone.

The tall screens above her blazed back to life, bombarding Kris with musical titles and ads. Kris ducked and huddled on the ground. Color and noise were everywhere. She stared upward and marveled at the sight; this was what Times Square had been like before the world changed.

Except the streets were empty—empty except for the orb.

The noise in her head was getting louder. It hurt, and she feared she would collapse under its weight. A million rock bands were playing all at once. It grew even stronger, and she cried out. There were voices too—many voices. She focused on them, trying to pull one thread from the chaotic black sea of voices. Kris touched her ears, expecting them to be bleeding, but her hands came away clean.

"We...are...many," the voices drawled.

She could hear those three words clearly now. They resolved

in her mind like craters on the moon coming into focus through a telescope. She forced the other noise aside and curled into the fetal position, her eyes closed, rocking slowly back and forth, unaware of anything else around her. She concentrated with all her strength on the words.

The voices weren't speaking in English or any other language. They were coded, like the message on the orb. The aliens were talking in pure mathematical constructs, yet Kris could understand them with effort.

Responding was difficult but possible. Her words came out haltingly, as if she were learning the rudiments of a foreign tongue. "We...no harm," she managed. "We...talk."

"We are listening." The voices were deeper and colder now, like a blast of arctic wind. They coalesced into a single voice with no gender. It was clear that the aliens used mathematical language as their primary form of communication. The roar in Kris's mind was becoming softer, losing intensity with each passing second. She was able to sit up now, though her head still felt as if it were made of lead.

A showering cascade of lights danced in her mind. They moved in slow patterns, breaking apart and reforming. The aliens were *talking* to her.

"Yes. Help us. Return...Mom," Kris said in her mind.

"Stored."

It took minutes for Kris to respond. Each word, each syllable, was a mountain she struggled to climb. Maybe they were saying that the people who'd vanished had been moved to a different space, a sideways part of the universe, rather than being killed. She hoped they were unharmed.

"I'm also...*stored*?" She struggled to translate her words into mathematical concepts.

"Yes," the drawling voices said.

Kris's hands shook. It was so unreal. The aliens had stored her in a pocket universe, as if she were in a science fiction movie.

"Why are you here?" Kris's mind felt so slow in this language;

she was like a toddler, learning to speak for the first time. Her head still reverberated with the sound, but clarity was emerging.

"Waiting."

"Why take…people?"

"Sorting," the voices said.

Their words baffled Kris. "I don't understand."

"Sorting," the voices repeated.

It took a moment, and then the answer flashed in Kris's mind. They wanted to find the ones who could speak to them. They were sorting the millions of humans into those who could speak to them and those who couldn't. No one in Sankofa Square had spoken back in mathematics, so the aliens had moved them into storage to get at the people who would be their translators. People like Kris.

"*Maker.* Speak the…" The word that followed was unintelligible.

There was silence, like Kris was in a giant empty cavern.

"I have questions," she finally said.

"We also have one." The statement was absolute.

Only one question? She was afraid to ask.

"Come to the nexus?" the orb asked.

"Nexus? What is that?"

There was no answer.

It struck Kris how odd this situation was. She was talking to a voice in her head in a mathematical language only she understood. The aliens were asking her to leave Earth to join them. But there were so many reasons to say no. She thought of her mom, her work, and her daily life. She also thought of Antoinette, who'd always encouraged her to be curious, bold, fearless. Something inside Kris pushed her forward. Maybe it was her insatiable curiosity. Maybe it was some unknown recklessness she didn't know she had. Maybe it was the hope that she could pull her mom from the nexus and bring her back home.

Whatever it was, Kris mustered up her courage. She didn't feel like she was in danger, although she was unbalanced. Her legs wobbled, and her head reeled from the bellowing voices. It was as if she were standing on the edge of a chasm, ready to jump off into a hazy unknown.

"Take me to the nexus," she said in her mind.

An answer came immediately. "Yes."

Kris walked around the orb one last time, soaking in the sights of Times Square. So much for her dream of going to New York. Though technically her dream had come true. And now she'd see much more.

The orb grew and moved toward her. She resisted stepping back and let it envelop her. The surface of it passed over her like a light curtain of water. She was inside the orb. Kris peered out at her surroundings. They were dimmer, like she was looking through tinted sunglasses. The dream from days ago surfaced again.

Freedom. Elation.

There was a flash.

Kris stumbled backward, falling into a new but faintly familiar place. But it was *no place*. She wasn't standing but floating, as if she were in the deep end of a limitless pool. Strange patterns rippled around her, moving in waves and lines like the images on the surface of the orbs.

She gasped, shivering from awe, though her surroundings were neither hot nor cold.

Something moved around her: ancient machines of impossible complexity. A scaffold-like building stretched in every direction, connecting the machines to tubular structures that glowed with a soft yellow light. The machines changed form, as if they were growing crystals or evolving fractals in a mathematical simulation. A nearby machine stopped and scanned her, its metallic body glimmering with countless reflections. Then it moved away again as if Kris were nothing but a momentary distraction.

The orbs were there too. Not one or ten, but millions in every direction. They were not black, featureless spheres here but glowing white stars pulsing with light. They spoke to each other in their mathematical language, and Kris wasn't sure how, but she could both hear and understand them. The orbs hovered around her, an infinite number of them stretching out to the horizon in every direction.

This was the nexus—the interdimensional space between an infinite number of parallel universes. She was in no place but connected to every place. Doorways led to other doorways in every direction. This was where the orbs lived, a place where physics didn't work the way humanity expected.

Kris heard their song now. There was a chorus of a million voices, neither male nor female, swirling around her in intricate harmonies.

Kris focused on an object that looked like a white braid—not one like Antoinette would put in her hair, but one made of *thoughts*. The structure was at the edge of her vision, but it grabbed her attention. She squinted to make out its features. It was a crack in space and time that she could look through to see other places. The fissure sent out ripples, folding in on itself.

She couldn't describe what she saw. But she saw.

There were worlds and people inside from the past and the future. Not people like her. But *others*. Kris's breath came fast as she tried to take it all in.

"There aren't enough poets to describe this," Kris said.

Sarah was there, a small fragment inside the braid. The rest of the vanished people were there too, along with untold millions of others, suspended in time like flies in amber. Kris tried to reach in and pull out her mother, but the braid was too far away.

She wanted to stay in this infinite expanse forever. The answers she'd striven for her whole life revealed themselves one by one, awakening like a child's newfound consciousness. She could see mathematical truths embedded in the intertwined threads of light like vibrations on a string, humming the orbs' communal song. All the mathematics she'd learned, every bit that she knew, was but one small piece in a larger pattern. Kris could see them all now, the patterns aligning into one of indescribable beauty.

Kris felt like she was dreaming. She closed her eyes, her head vibrating. She could see the braid even through her closed eyelids, growing in intensity as she watched it. She opened her eyes, and they blurred with tears. She put her hands to her ears as if to block out an inaudible roar. No human had ever seen what she was seeing.

"You cannot stay," the orbs said.

Kris wanted to join with the white braid, merge with it.

"You are not ready. Maker must bring the pattern we seek."

She yearned to stay. She was infinite, dissolving into the braid. She wanted to beg them. She would give anything.

Kris was pulled upward, as if giant arms were lifting her from the bottom of the sea. She tried to resist, but like a baby being lifted from a warm bath, she could do nothing.

Her eyes opened, and she was back in Times Square. She was on Earth. Antoinette held her as she looked up at the stars peppering the sky between the dark towers.

"Wake up, K! We can't stay here!"

Antoinette's face blurred into a dancing parade of dots and lines. Kris put her hand on the ground, feeling the coolness of the concrete under her fingers. The ground felt electric. The world was a single equation that made perfect sense.

Kris drank it in. Although she stood on solid ground, it shifted under her. Even standing still, she was carried by it, as if the world were moving fast enough to make her dizzy. Looking up, the planet turned beneath her, rushing through space. The solar system orbited the supermassive black hole at the galaxy's center, one more rotation in the system. She closed her eyes and waited for the feeling to pass.

"I saw it—the nexus. I've got to tell the others," Kris said. Her voice was shaky, and her body vibrated from her journey to the orb's home.

"You were right in front of the freakin' orb for twenty minutes, standing there like a statue. You didn't move at all."

Kris shook her head. She'd been gone for only a few minutes, and she'd vanished from the square to visit the nexus.

"Am I gonna have to carry you out of here?"

Kris put a finger to Antoinette's lips to quiet her. Ari stood next to them, quietly watching with his arms folded. In the dim starlight, his eyes looked like Toor's.

Kris reached for her bag and pulled out her diary, fingers trembling as she flipped to a blank page. She pulled a pen out of her pocket and scratched equations onto the white paper, squinting as she struggled to get them right: a system of differential equations that modeled the orb's home, the infinite-dimensional space they'd built. The symbols came to her as if dictated. They made a kind of sense, but less so with each passing second. The memory of that place was receding like the tide. She could still see it, but the details were blurry.

The world around her resolved itself back to normal. Kris felt tiny and disconnected. There was her breath once again, rising and falling in rhythmic pants. She stared at the equations and committed them to memory. Then she sat up, leaning on her sister.

"We gotta go," Ari said.

"What the hell happened to you?" Antoinette asked.

"Hey! You there!" a voice shouted.

Awakening from her reverie, Kris turned to see a soldier running toward them from across the street. Panicked, Antoinette pulled Kris to her feet, and they ran past the orb toward Ari, who was beckoning them. Kris's whole body shook as she rushed to leave this place. She threw her diary into her bag and clutched it to her tightly.

Ari yanked Kris around the corner. Antoinette was right behind them. Kris's legs seized and a groan escaped her before Ari could get a hand over her mouth.

"Quiet, now," Ari whispered. They moved behind a dumpster. Antoinette stood rigid and scared a few feet away, her hands clenched into fists. There was nothing they could do now but hide. Helplessness overwhelmed Kris.

The soldier who'd been pursuing them walked, stopping to peer around with a flashlight. Antoinette remained silent, her eyes locked on Kris's. There was a noise like a car door closing in the distance, and the soldier ran off.

"Come on! I saw a place nearby where we can hide," Ari said in a low hiss.

"Let's get out of here," Antoinette said.

Kris was sweating all over, breathing fast, her heart racing. Her knees went weak, and she had to steady herself.

The three of them ran down the dark streets, past abandoned cars, kicking up litter as they fled. Kris looked over her shoulder. No one was chasing them. Ari vanished into a dark doorway, and they followed him down a long hall lit by a red exit sign.

The wind picked up outside the window, and the sound jolted Kris into the present. Antoinette sat next to her, her phone lighting up her face. The place was dark and filled with musty brown boxes marked with white labels. She had no idea what time it was, but she ached with fatigue.

"I don't think the soldier followed us. He would've found us by now," Antoinette said. In the faint light, Kris could make out Ari sitting next to them, eyes closed, as if he were sleeping or meditating.

"Where are we?" she asked.

"From what I can tell, it seems like the back storage room of a tacky souvenir shop. You crashed as soon as we came inside. Passed out, maybe. I dunno."

Kris pulled herself up with effort. Her head throbbed, and she saw little white sparks behind her eyes when she moved. The world tilted, and she wanted to throw up. Antoinette reached out and grabbed her forehead. Her hands were cold and clammy. Kris gagged but didn't vomit.

"I'm putting an end to this mess," Antoinette said. "I'm calling Toor, if I can get service. Hopefully, Ms. CIA and her MIB goons will show up before some rogue weirdo attacks us."

Ari's eyes opened. "We should do what Antoinette says. It's probably best if I try to text her," he said.

Antoinette lifted her chin. "I wish you'd listened to me before you went all rogue, Dumbo Ears. Go ahead, then, and call Mommy CIA," she said with venom.

"Stop calling my mom and me names. All I did was touch the orb like Kris," he said. Antoinette stuck out her tongue.

Kris was so weak, she wanted nothing more than to lie down again. She coughed. "Mom. Sarah..." Cold sweat trickled down her temples and back.

Antoinette pulled her back down, and the two sat facing each other. "Go on. What about her?"

"The aliens said she's stored with the others."

"What do you mean, *stored*? The vanished people from Toronto and here? You saw them?"

"Not exactly." Her words came out in spurts. "It was like seeing the world inside out. The orbs took me to where they live. They call it the nexus. I don't think I could explain it, even if I tried. But when I was there, things made sense. All of it. Math, I mean. Not just symbols...but why they matter. They said Mom and the others were stored there. I saw her. I felt her."

Hot tears ran down Kris's cheeks. Even though she couldn't articulate the experience or even remember it with precision, she could feel it in her body. The beauty and scope of what she'd seen were beyond imagining. The whole world she knew, full of people and cars and houses, was a faint candle compared to the overpowering radiance of that place.

"If you think Mom was there, wherever the hell you were, then we've got to go back. Back to the orb," Antoinette said.

"I didn't see any of that. The orb just turned red when I

touched it and blew me backward," Ari said, rubbing his shoulder. Antoinette glared at him. But how had he made time slow and stop? None of it made sense to Kris.

"No, I can't go back. They said I'm not ready. That I have to return with the patterns," Kris said.

"What patterns?" Ari asked, leaning forward.

"We've got to decode the aliens' message." It was a test. A cosmic exam. Kris's eyelids fluttered, and she swallowed hard to avoid retching.

"Shhh, sis. We're gonna wait this shitstorm out until Toor and her crew come and get us. Not sure we should have come here alone. But at least the sun will be up soon."

"Mom's safe. The orbs have her with the others, I promise," Kris said, her voice faint.

Antoinette stroked her hair. Kris shot a glance at Ari. He hesitated and then crossed his arms. There was a shifty look in his eyes, like he was hiding something. It made the hairs on the back of Kris's neck stand up.

A dull thud came from outside the blackened doorway. Kris jumped. The red light of the exit sign loomed ominously above the door. Voices sounded, and then the door creaked open. Soldiers wearing black clothes and masks funneled in like ants pouring out of a hole, guns at the ready. Kris curled into a ball and hid her head in her hands.

Toor entered and shone a light at Kris and Antoinette. She cleared her throat. "Are you hurt, Dr. Argentia?"

Kris looked up, too overwhelmed to speak. She shook her head. Toor offered her hand, and Kris took it. It was cold but strong.

"I'm fine too, Mother, thanks for asking," Ari said with a smirk.

"We traced your location from your phone. Now...Kris, we need you back. Every minute that passes is another minute we don't know the truth about the message." Toor paused. "Did you make contact with the orb?"

Kris tensed. She remained silent. Toor glanced at Antoinette, whose arms were folded. Kris clenched her teeth.

"Don't look at me, Madam CIA," said Antoinette.

"The three of you have nothing to say for yourselves? You snuck off the base in the middle of the night, stowed away in a truck, and found your way to Times Square just for kicks?"

"Sounds about right. Why don't you pick on people your own age?" Antoinette snarled.

"I touched the orb, and it communicated with me," Kris said.

Toor's eyes narrowed. She pulled up a screen on the wall of the storage room. "This is the footage we have of your encounter with the orb. We have a camera trained on it at all times."

The image was grainy, but Kris saw herself standing next to the orb. Antoinette stood frozen behind her, as she remembered. There was a blank expression on her face, and her eyes were closed. Kris shook her head in disbelief.

"We have approximately twenty minutes of footage with you standing there, not moving," Toor said.

"I know, Antoinette told me. But I only remember being away for a few minutes." She shot a glance at Antoinette and scratched her nose.

Toor was silent for a few long seconds and then narrowed her eyes. "It's time we got back to the base."

The sun was rising as Kris and Antoinette followed Toor and the soldiers back out to the street. The light made Kris blink, and she held a hand over her eyes as she and Antoinette got into the blacked-out SUV that was to take them back to the base. Toor and Ari would follow in another car soon. He shouted goodbye to Kris, and she waved in return.

"It's hard to imagine all those displaced people out there. There are millions of them, many fending for themselves," Kris said. The immensity of it sent a shiver through her.

Kris tried to sleep as the SUV rumbled through the vacant streets of Manhattan, but she couldn't. Every time she closed her eyes, the orb's patterns darted like fireflies across her lids. Her breath came quick as she concentrated on the message and its meaning. Garbled ideas ran through her brain like the labyrinth of a budding proof, only this time she couldn't make sense of anything. She was lost in her mind. She knew that if she just tried harder, the solution would come. The M-Team had to decode the alien flashes, or they were all done for.

Kris already had a vague map of the message, so it was a matter of piecing the details together. As with the Riemann hypothesis, she could sit for days, pulling the threads together, gathering the strands to make a perfect braid of new mathematics.

The aliens viewed people as small and easily overlooked. They must be so advanced that to them, humans were like tiny bugs scurrying around the planet. They'd sent the orbs, so that meant they were willing to communicate, but on their terms.

The problem is, we're too stupid to talk to them, she thought.

Kris began to drift off as they made their way down the empty highways back to the base.

After a while, her phone rang and she jolted. There had been no connection. Or so she'd believed. She opened Rix, and Nate's face popped up on the screen, rigid with anger.

"You can't go off like that. I was wild with worry," he said, his sharp brown eyes glaring.

"I know. It was stupid."

Kris didn't say anything more about what she'd learned in front of the driver. She'd fill in Nate and Toor when she got back to the base. For now, she kept it to herself.

CHAPTER 7

WORLD UNRAVELS

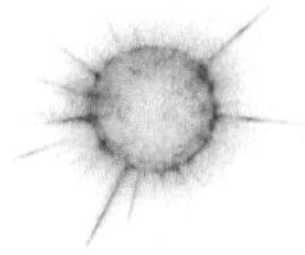

K RIS WALKED THE *empty streets of Toronto. An unseen force had sucked all the life from the city. In the center of Sankofa Square, the orb pulsed, broadcasting its message toward the sky. Kris walked alone through the barren streets, looking for something but not sure what. She had to keep away from the orb.*

"You are not ready," its voices bellowed in chorus.

She ran. Ran until she couldn't breathe, panting so hard she had to lean on the wall of one of the vacant buildings.

FLASH.

An infinite field. Beneath her feet, wild green grass grew, rough and wavy like uncombed hair. She looked up and squinted to make out the vision emerging above. A single orb hovered in the sky. This one was different from the others, larger. It was the size of a football field, glowing red and pulsing.

Kris ran as fast as she could, but black dots began to emerge at the horizon line. Dozens of orbs, growing in size as they moved closer. Invisible lines connected them like a network in the sky. Kris was missing something, but she couldn't remember what. What am I looking for?

"Not ready," said the voices.

She couldn't outrun them. Everywhere she looked, orbs filled the sky. Thousands of them, blocking out the sun. Pulsing. Growing louder every second.

Kris woke with a start in the back of the SUV. Antoinette was sleeping. Her phone said it was seven a.m. on Thursday morning.

The car jostled over the uneven, muddy road leading to a checkpoint. Kris had no idea where they were, but it wasn't the base. The driver rolled his window down, and the sun beamed onto Kris's cheeks. He flashed his identification card at the guard, and the soldier waved them on. The smell of diesel lingered in the air as the window resealed.

"Where're we going?" Kris asked the driver.

"You'll see. We're taking a detour as ordered by Agent Toor."

They emerged into a bleak landscape Kris already knew. Rows of heavy cloth tents stretched out for miles before them, green fabric rustling in the wind. Hundreds of people shuffled between the rows, interspersed with the guards stationed there. The SUV slowed and then stopped. Kris roused Antoinette as the driver stepped out and came around to open their door. Antoinette exited first. Kris slid out of the SUV to stand beside her. There was flattened grass under her feet. The military had converted a field into one enormous campsite. The driver then told them to wait.

Toor's car pulled up, and she hopped out, followed by Ari. He squinted in the sun and said nothing, staying close to Toor's side. Kris could see her reflection in the woman's sunglasses.

"Welcome to Camp 1123, containing twenty-nine thousand, seven hundred and eighty-four refugees from Manhattan," Toor said.

Kris and Antoinette walked up and down the rows of tents with Toor. They heard children playing in a tent that was functioning as a daycare. Another with a half-open flap contained people sleeping. A few tents were empty, but most were full.

"Because of the orbs' arrival, there are now countless places like these, not only here and in Toronto but in dozens of major cities around the world. Amazing that they pulled all of this together in only three days. It's the biggest recorded refugee crisis in history," Toor said.

It had only been days, though the scale of the upheaval made it feel like weeks had already passed. Kris and Antoinette exchanged glances as they moved past a tent with an elderly man and woman inside. The man's eyes caught Kris's; there was sorrow there, and loss.

"I wanted you to see this with your own eyes, Kris. Now you know what's happening in the world as the M-Team works in the safety of our base."

Kris swallowed hard, her throat parched. The beaming sun made her dizzy. She couldn't imagine living in one of those tents, baking in the July sun.

"You made your friggin' point. Now let's get out of here," Antoinette said.

"Kris Argentia?" The voice was soft, so small amid the endless rows of tents framed by the blue sky and the burning sunshine. It was a girl no older than ten, her red hair pulled back in a ponytail. "You're one of the M-Team. You want this?" the girl asked, holding out a bottle of water.

Kris reached for it even as her fingers shook. This girl lost so much, and yet she was trying to help Kris.

I'm so selfish. I'm doing math while she suffers in this place, Kris thought.

There were a million girls like this stuck in camps all over the world, waiting for someone to save them. And if the M-Team couldn't help, if Kris couldn't help, then no one could.

The feeling of guilt surged through her once again, making her body ache. She had to get away. Blood pounded in Kris's ears. Her hands shook and her feet tingled.

Kris ran.

She sprinted away from the girl, from Toor, even from her sister. She ran so fast she lost track of her location. Rows and rows of tents extended in every direction, like the infinite sea of orbs in her dream. And just like in the dream, she couldn't outrun them. There were too many.

Kris slumped to the ground, defeated, her lungs burning. She put her head in her hands and tried to block out the sights and smells of the tents and the people.

Then there were arms around her, pulling her up. It was Antoinette. Kris leaned on her, her arms and legs weak and wobbly. Ari ran over to grasp Kris's free left hand. His hand was sweaty and hot.

"I've got you, K," Antoinette said. Toor stood nearby, watching the scene through her black sunglasses. Antoinette turned to her. "We need to go back. Enough of this drama."

As they found their way back to the SUV, a small crowd gathered. Young and old, fat and thin, rich and poor. They were ordinary people. And they were displaced, with many missing loved ones. Silence met Kris as she shuffled by. The girl who'd given her the water held her mother's hand.

Kris looked away as she climbed into the back of the SUV. The driver closed the door and rolled the tinted windows up.

Kris glanced at Antoinette and grabbed her hand. "This is bigger than me. It's not only for Mom. It's for all of us," she whispered.

"You gotta see this. I've got service," Antoinette said.

Kris stirred in the back seat of the SUV. Her eyelids were droopy, and she wanted to curl into a ball and not move for a week. The driver was watching a vid on Rix while the car drove itself along the empty highway. She focused on Antoinette's phone, which was playing a news stream.

"The aliens want us to *love them*," Yolanda Choi said.

Yolanda was an internet superstar at just eighteen years old with millions of followers on Rix. Self-professed queen of fabulousness, she gave viewers total access to her day-to-day activities. She held a white Pomeranian who was unfazed by the cameras and paparazzi. Her bodyguards kept curious onlookers at a safe distance, and the news anchor's voiceover explained that she was en route to a safe place that her father—a general in the army—had arranged. She was too famous to stay in the camps; it would cause too much commotion.

Kris laughed as she watched the clip on the small screen. Yolanda wore a red sequined dress with white fur around the neck—fake, of course. She pushed a lock of auburn hair out of her eyes, tucking it back behind her ear as the paparazzi's cameras flashed away. Her tanned skin contrasted with her giant white hat and oversized sunglasses. A reporter asked her what she would say to the aliens.

"I'm all about love and understanding. It says a lot about our universe that beings, even from other galaxies, are still searching for that. The M-Team is working on how to talk to the aliens. All we can do is hope they'll find an answer soon. I'm going to meet with them to offer my support."

She smiled for the cameras, pulling her sunglasses down. Her dark brown eyes met the lenses, steady and serene.

For a second, she forgot how to breathe. Yolanda was coming to the base. She was the same age as Antoinette, only two years older than Kris, but she might as well have come from a different world. Kris traveled between home and the university a few kilometers away. Yolanda bounced around the globe.

"Can you say where you're going?" asked one photographer.

"No, I can't say. I'll be back before you know it, though. My stream will be on a brief hiatus, but remember, I am forever and ever your Yolanda."

By late afternoon, they were back at the base. Toor and Ari disappeared as soon as they arrived. Kris was so tired her bones ached. The emotional wallop of the visit to the camp on top of her experience with the orbs made her head spin. She had to make amends with Nate, then reapply herself to the message. She knew

Nate was freaking out, but surely he would forgive her when he learned the truth about why she'd left. She had to explain what she'd learned from the aliens.

Serendipitously, he was the first to meet her as she climbed out of the SUV and trudged through the dust of the base's courtyard.

"You were so reckless. We searched everywhere for you and Antoinette," he said, his eyes bulging.

"Sorry. I wanted to tell you, but I knew you wouldn't let me go."

Nate cleared his throat. "Toor gave me an update, but she wants to debrief with you in one hour. I stuck my neck out defending your place on the M-Team after this fiasco. Please don't be late," Nate said. He turned with a sigh and walked away.

Kris's body ached, and her eyes were blurry from fatigue. She collapsed into her bed and cuddled into her pillow. She kept sneezing—maybe she'd caught a cold. She curled up in the fetal position and closed her eyes, but still she couldn't rest. All she could see was the flashing patterns of the orb.

A hot shower revived Kris. Her damp hair clung to her neck as she walked with Antoinette into Toor's office. The walls were white and barren like everywhere else on the base, and the room was empty except for a desk with a tablet and some chairs. Nate and Ari sat on the right side of the white desk opposite Kris and Antoinette. Ari looked at the floor, and his expression betrayed an inner turmoil like Niagara Falls. Kris's stomach tightened.

When everyone was seated, Toor began, clear and direct as usual. "Thank you, Kris, Antoinette, and Ari, for coming to this meeting. We're not here to lay blame or recrimination but rather to learn what we can from your interactions with the orb."

"Are we in the principal's office?" Antoinette asked. Kris elbowed her in the arm, and she scowled.

"It was me," Kris said. "I take responsibility. I convinced Ant to come with me, and Ari followed us."

"As Toor said, we're not here to punish you. We need information," Nate said.

"*The nexus*," Kris said. Toor's face went pale as she said those words. Nate's face was open. Kris sat back in her chair and cleared her throat. "The orbs showed me a place called the nexus, where they live." Kris remembered her encounter with the orb, trying to piece together her words.

It was strange, beautiful. Otherworldly.

There was a long silence.

"Are you sure it wasn't a hallucination? You're prone to this kind of thing, what with your math trances," Nate said.

"No. This was real," Kris said.

Nate scratched his chin and squinted. "I'd theorize that the aliens drop orbs flashing their message on a planet with a sufficiently advanced species. Our rover on Mars got their attention. Perhaps they wanted evidence we can travel off-world?" he said.

"That may be true, but we have no other evidence to back it up. Kris, can you describe the nexus? We understand that from your perspective, you vanished from Times Square and time began to move at a different rate," Toor said.

"I think that's what happened. I don't have the right words to describe the place they took me. It was like diving deep into the ocean, but at a certain point I came up for air on the other side. I suppose I was in a pocket universe, or at least my mind was there. Or probably so," Kris said.

"This makes no sense," Toor said.

"It's just basic non-Euclidean geometry," Kris said.

"Yes, I see. If the aliens live in an extra-dimensional, compact Riemannian manifold, then it makes a certain sense. The extra dimensions would allow the orbs to pop in and out of space anywhere they choose. They moved Kris into a pocket universe adjacent to ours," Nate said.

"If this makes any less sense, I'm going to need a map," Antoinette said.

Toor shook her head. "You've lost me again, too."

"I'm going to regret asking," Ari said, "but how can you travel to another universe?"

"Think of space like a flat sheet of paper," Nate said. He grabbed a scrap of paper from the table. "We can only move across it. But if that sheet exists in a higher dimension, it can fold."

He bent the paper, bringing two distant corners together.

"Parts that are far apart suddenly touch. The orbs aren't crossing our universe the long way. They're slipping into small pocket universes that sit right next to ours, then popping back out somewhere else."

No one spoke. Ari cleared his throat.

"I've been dreaming about the orbs," Ari said, looking from face to face. Toor's eyes narrowed, and her back straightened. "I tried to make contact with one, but it rejected me. The aliens wanted to talk to me. They called me the *Maker*."

"They called me that too, and I don't know what that means. They said I wasn't ready and that I had to return with the patterns they wanted," Kris said.

"It's the *message* they're after," Nate said. "It has to be about deciphering the message playing on the orbs. That's what they want us to do."

Kris pulled out a piece of paper covered with dense formulas and gave it to Nate.

"She wrote that in her diary right after she touched the orb," Antoinette said.

His eyes bulged. "My god, what is this? I've never seen equations of this kind. Kris, where did you get these?"

"I don't know. I remember writing them down and memorizing them. When I was in the nexus, I could understand the equations, but after I left, I only remembered bits and pieces. Their meaning was all fuzzy, which is odd for me, because when I learn an equation, it quickly becomes an old friend."

"And you saw Mom?" Antoinette asked.

"Yeah, and the others—the people who vanished from Toronto and New York City. But only for a brief instant. The orbs said they were stored."

"Tell us more about that," Toor said. She leaned toward Kris.

"It wasn't like I could see Mom and the other vanished people as I see you now. They were suspended. It was as if I could *feel* them," Kris said. The hair on her arms stood up as she spoke.

"That's good news. At least it means they aren't dead," Nate said.

Toor blinked and pushed back her chair. "If Kris's account is accurate, then this confirms some of our theories. The M-Team must double down on deciphering the message. Perhaps these equations will play a vital role. Wallace, I want you to share them with the M-Team. Tell them what happened to Kris in the nexus."

Nate clasped his hands together, squeezing them once, hard. His gaze dropped to the table. "And I want the rest of you to get some sleep. Kris, I'm sorry for the intrusion, but we will be monitoring your location from now on. You can't leave the base like that again. The stakes are too high. Ari, you're forbidden to interact with Kris and Antoinette. There will be no more rogue road trips under my watch. This meeting is over."

Ari let out a long breath.

Losing her freedom to roam was a logical punishment.

"How're you feeling?" Antoinette asked Kris as they left the office.

"Like I've run a marathon, and then someone kicked me in the shin, and then I got the mother of all migraines. Otherwise, I'm fine."

Antoinette linked arms with her. "Do you think deciphering the message will get Mom back?"

"I hope so. There are no other options left," Kris said.

Kris's stomach growled around midnight. She was hungry enough to eat a pickle sandwich. Groggy and off-balance, she'd never make it until morning without something to eat. She opened the door and was startled to see a soldier standing in the corridor.

"All okay, Dr. Argentia?"

"Um, yeah. I was going to the mess hall to see if I could find something to eat."

"Not a problem, but I'm under orders to supervise you while you're on the base."

"Toor's orders?"

The soldier nodded. He was probably only in his early twenties. Kris wondered how he'd become a soldier, what threads of his life had led him here to the base, guarding her.

"Yes, Toor's orders. Private Randy Dax, at your service." He nodded once.

As they walked toward the mess hall, Kris heard a thumping noise that grew louder as they approached. She could hardly believe the sight she saw when Dax pushed the door open for her.

"Hello, Daddy. Hello, Mom!"

Antoinette and Yolanda, who was still dressed in her white sequined dress, were screaming like banshees over loud music. Kris recognized the song from Antoinette's classic rock collection from a million years ago: "Cherry Bomb" by the Runaways, featuring Joan Jett. It had always been one of Antoinette's favorites.

"I'm your ch-ch-ch-ch-ch-ch-ch-cherry bomb!"

A tiny white Pomeranian ran around the hall, barking frantically as the two girls shouted into the spoons they were using as microphones.

"Ant! Hey, Ant!" Kris waved her arms to no effect. She ran toward the pair, and when Antoinette noticed her, she threw her arm around Kris, holding the spoon to her mouth.

"I'm your ch-ch-ch-ch-ch-ch-ch-cherry bomb!" Kris screamed.

Private Dax looked on, perplexed. He pulled at his collar and his sleeves, clearly unsure what he should do. When the song finished, Yolanda and Antoinette slumped to the ground, exhausted but exhilarated after their performance.

"Hi, I'm Yolanda." Her eyes were dangerous black pools of quicksand. Kris blushed. It was as if ETC's sister had come for a visit. Yolanda was even more fabulous in person than on Rix.

"I know who you are," Kris said. "You're famous. I've seen your stream a million times."

"Of course you have. Everyone knows me. This is Cindi, spelled with an *i*," she said as the Pomeranian licked Kris's outstretched fingers.

"I'm Kris. Your pup is so cute," Kris said. She'd never met a dog she didn't like.

"We were blowing off some steam. It's kinda boring here if you're not a soldier or a mathematician," Antoinette said. Yolanda stretched out on the floor, lifting Cindi above her and making faces.

"Why are you here, if you don't mind me asking?" Kris said.

"Long story, but I'll make it short. I was in my loft in Brooklyn when it happened. I mean, I could see the waves of people coming over the bridges from my windows. I watched them vanish." Yolanda paused. "It was terrifying. Dad was in Washington, and they had closed all the airports. I would have caused a riot if I'd gone to a camp, so Dad figured I'd be safer here. It was the closest base. You're part of the M-Team; you were on Rix. You guys are big shots or something."

"This is so friggin' cool. I'm hanging with Yolanda," Antoinette said.

Kris grabbed a green apple from the giant stainless-steel fridge, said good night, and retreated to her room, munching on the way. The apple was cold and crunchy and sour. The AC gave her a chill, and she grabbed her favorite sweater, the red one with a zipper. She turned off the lights except for the one by her bed and opened her phone. It was time to visit with her Gal Pals.

The last message Toor had sent was short and somewhat cryptic.

Argentia contacted the orb. Waiting for additional orders.

A lump rose in Kris's throat. She closed her eyes and tried to think. *What orders? Wasn't Toor the boss of this whole show?*

Worst case, maybe Toor knew about Kris's breach of her files. But that was unlikely—Kris was careful to cover her tracks. She wasn't sure she trusted Toor.

She tapped an icon. An image of her and Sarah projected on the wall. They were smiling, and the sun was shining. She had caught a glimpse of her mother in the nexus. Kris was going to get her back, whatever it took, even if it meant following Nate's every order. Deciphering the message was the one surefire way.

She stared at the image and couldn't look away.

Kris's eyes adjusted to the faint light from her charging phone. She tapped it—she'd slept for seven hours, and it was Friday morning. The deep sleep had worked wonders; patterns were lining up. All she needed now was a strong coffee and a shower.

The return to the M-Team was going to be awkward. Kris wasn't sure Nate had forgiven her for running away, but she would try again to explain why she'd done it. His main focus had to be deciphering the message. She'd play it cool and find common ground with the other mathematicians.

Her diary called out to her, and she wrote in it with her favorite black pen. The memory of Times Square lingered, already fading at the edges. But it had been only a day. She wasn't sure what she'd witnessed. At the very least, the orb was a super-advanced piece of technology. Kris couldn't fathom how the aliens must view humans if they could easily send these silent emissaries to so many other worlds.

Friday, July 20, 2035. This is how they make first contact, she wrote. As soon as they find a species sophisticated enough, they start dropping orbs in the major cities. Nate even said something like that. It's like a cosmic welcome mat, though a sinister one.

I can feel the orb's patterns. I can't see them in my mind's eye anymore; they're buried, but I can feel them moving.

In other news, I met Yolanda, and Ari is off-limits. Ugh, pickle sandwiches for everyone.

Kris yawned wide and stretched. She put her diary in a drawer of the desk and opened a screen with her work on the orb's message. She grappled with her last serious work on the message.

"The equations I wrote in my diary in Times Square could be enough to get us somewhere," she mumbled to herself. She waited a few minutes while the program ran through a few million deciphering codes based on her ideas. Nothing. Her work looked the same as it had before, the ten symmetrical chunks she'd discovered days ago.

She didn't understand. The new equations should change *something*.

The M-Team shared their ideas in a private folder only the group could see, although Kris figured that Toor was also watching every move they made. The team had been hard at work. Reams of data from hundreds of groups around the world, all of whom had been working to decipher the message, filled her screen. But as she scrolled through their work, there was no progress. The problem was too complex for a glorified calculator to solve.

Kris arrived at the mess hall in the morning and ate alone, Private Dax standing by her side. Yolanda came in next, Cindi in her purse. The soldiers having breakfast walked up to shake her hand and get her autograph. "Now, now, boys and girls. You have to make way for Cindi and me to get our morning coffee. Oh, Kris! Hi!"

Cindi licked Kris's hand as Yolanda sat next to her. The bright lights revealed the symmetry of her face.

"I've always wanted a dog," said Kris. "When this is all over, maybe we can adopt one."

"She likes you. That's something special, you know—she doesn't warm up to strangers quickly. Are you eating that?" Yolanda pointed to the toast on Kris's plate. Without waiting for an answer, she picked it up and fed it to Cindi. Kris blinked. Apparently the answer was no.

"Poor little darling is starving. I hope they have the special food I requested for her."

"Aren't you going to have breakfast?" Kris asked.

"No, only coffee. Black. I eat only once a day. It's important how many times a day you eat."

Kris said, "Oh," because there didn't seem to be a correct response.

The two of them sat there in silence for a while until Yolanda spoke again. "The service here is so slow."

"You have to get your own coffee. It's a cafeteria," Kris said.

"I'll get it," Private Dax said, and jogged toward the coffee maker like it was part of his training.

"Boys. They're all the same. I haven't dated one in ages," Yolanda said.

"I wouldn't know. I've never dated anyone."

"You can enter dateville when you're older."

Kris continued, "There was a graduate student, Shawn, who came to study with Nate. We chatted after every number theory seminar and went out for the occasional coffee on campus. But I can't really call those dates. Maybe he took pity on me because I was younger than the other students, or maybe he liked my math.

I liked him a lot. He taught me a few Ojibwe words. We mostly lost touch after that, but we follow each other."

"It must be tough being so smart and so young."

Kris stammered, "I-I suppose so. I don't have a normal life."

Yolanda caught her gaze. She put her hand on Kris's, which sent electric currents through her arm.

"Life hasn't always been easy for me either. I spent a lot of years moving around. My dad is a big-shot general. I was famous when I was younger than you—couldn't walk down the street without protection. That's why I'm here. It's supposed to be one of the safest places in the country with all of you here."

Yolanda waved at the soldiers pointing at her. One man asked Kris to take a photo of him with Yolanda. She was speechless as she tapped on the phone. She was one of the few experts who could help save the world, and she was playing paparazzo to Yolanda Choi.

Private Dax came back with the coffee. Yolanda thanked him, sipped it, and gave a slight scowl.

"Not so good. I'll get something salty to eat later. Hey, do you like salt? I *love* salt! I put too much of it on everything," Yolanda said. Her comments left Kris puzzled.

"I'd better go see Nate," she said. "We've got work to do on deciphering the message."

Yolanda winked a goodbye and pulled a few screens up on the table.

Kris left the mess hall, Private Dax trailing reluctantly behind her. Ari ducked into the mess hall after her. He followed Toor's orders and didn't stop to say hello.

Kris knocked on Nate's closed office door. After a long wait, he opened it. The contents shocked her. Scattered papers covered Nate's office, along with several half-drunk cups of coffee. He'd always been so neat and composed, but not now. He slouched in his chair, dark circles under his eyes. She sat and let him speak first.

He spoke in a frail voice. "I didn't sleep. I'm stuck. We're stuck.

We need your intellectual firepower on this. The stakes are as high as they could ever be," Nate said, glaring.

The weight of it pressed down on Kris's chest. She felt out of place, like he had her confused with someone braver, someone smarter. If he was counting on her, he didn't know how close she already felt to failing.

"I'll help however I can. I don't want us stuck like this. And I'll try to be better about working with everyone. I promise," Kris said, her stomach tightening.

Nate looked down at the table, then back at her. "I know you will," he said.

There was a knock on the door, and Toor entered. Without preamble, she said, "Another orb appeared. London."

Silence fell as the news sank in.

"Oh, $f(u)=c^k$," Kris whispered.

Kris walked into the workroom to discover Benedita there alone. "Are we early?" she asked as she looked around.

"Yes. The others should be here soon. I prefer the quiet, so I come early to work alone," Benedita said.

"Nate will be late—he's talking with Toor. Any more ideas?"

"Nada. We had a few small hunches, but the message is too complex. It's like random noise. By the way, Dr. Wallace said you're the most brilliant doctoral student he's ever had. I read your thesis on the Collatz problem. Incredible."

"Thanks. Nate is melodramatic, though. When did you get your doctorate?"

"Last year at Berkeley. I'm not sure what I'm doing here with all these famous mathematicians like you."

Nate did things for a reason. Benedita must have impressed him, and that was hard to do. Kris wondered if she should tell Benedita about her proof of the Riemann hypothesis. While it was tempting, she checked herself before saying anything; it wasn't the right time. Besides, Nate had made her promise not to tell other mathematicians.

"I'm the second youngest here, next to you. Twenty-three is still young to get a doctorate."

"Believe me, being a prodigy isn't as nice as you'd expect."

"They called me that too back home. I frightened the other children. Adults too."

"We have that in common," Kris said.

Speaking with Benedita was like talking to an older, wiser version of herself. It gave her confidence. Kris didn't have close friends other than Nate and her sister. But talking with Benedita felt natural. She had a quiet grace about her, as if she were lit from within. She wished she knew people like Benedita in Toronto so they could go out for coffee at The Uncommon and prove theorems together.

"But tell me, what was the orb like?" Benedita said, pulling her long black hair over one shoulder.

Just then, Nate arrived with the remaining members of the M-Team. He locked eyes with Kris, and the other team members greeted her.

"Toronto, New York, Beijing, and now London," said Nate. "Four orbs, and it's likely we'll see more. We need to get this message deciphered as soon as possible. At least we've got Kris's equations. Let me state that again in simple terms: Let's solve this goddamn thing!"

As far as motivational speeches went, Nate's left a lot to be desired. It was more like the chiding of an angry parent than the cheering of a pep squad. Regardless, everyone dove into work.

The day was long and trying. The group wasn't working well as a unit, and people often broke off into solitary islands. Every time Kris tried to steer them toward a common goal like deciphering her equations, it worked for a short time, but then the islands reformed and people went to work on their separate ideas.

By six p.m., Kris was feeling the effects of the intense day of thinking. She stretched her arms out and rubbed her neck. Nate stayed behind to work, but the rest of the team left for dinner. Benedita asked Kris to come with them, but she declined, even though her stomach was growling. She had to leave the workroom, though—she knew her limits, and she needed time to recharge her spent batteries. She visited Antoinette's quarters instead.

"Hey, K." Antoinette said.

"Ugh. I'm so tired. We can't seem to make any progress. We're at an impasse." Kris sat on the bed, where Antoinette was playing guitar. "Did you spend the day with Yolanda?"

"No. I'm chilling, mostly bored. I read and watched videos saved on my phone and stuff." Antoinette strummed her guitar, focusing on her chords.

There was a knock on the door, and Antoinette hopped up to open it. Yolanda stood on the other side.

"I need to do something—I'm so sick of being cooped up in these little closets. Toni, can I dye your hair blond? I know you're all Goth, but it would be fun."

"Apocalypse makeover. I'm in."

The two giggled as they left to gather supplies, leaving Kris behind. The "cool" girls did their thing while she worked on mathematics. The casual way Antoinette had talked about the world ending stung Kris like a cranky wasp. Didn't she and Yolanda grasp the terrible events happening? This wasn't some show on Rix—it was real.

Kris logged into Antoinette's display and scanned through the news sites available through the base's network. The situation was gloomy everywhere. The world was plummeting into chaos like Toor had said it would. Pakistan and India were close to a full-fledged war. The refugee camps were overflowing around every major city in Europe. There were riots over food in the US and Canada. The stock markets remained closed, and world economies were tanking.

The aliens hadn't attacked. They came from the sky. They took.

Kris narrowed her eyes, holding onto what pressed at her. Millions had been taken. What kind of advanced civilization would create this much misery? And if they wanted humans gone, why not erase us outright? It would be cleaner. Almost merciful compared to dragging it out like this.

Kris put her head in her hands as the news sites reported the appearance of yet another orb, this time in Mumbai. The day was unraveling fast. *Perhaps the world is ending*, she thought. The cold white walls of the room reflected only gloom.

Kris saw the white braid against the backdrop of a field of glowing orbs. The answers were all there. She could see the proof of the Riemann hypothesis curled inside it, like one jewel shining in an ocean of jewels. Sarah was there too, along with the millions of other vanished people.

"Bring us the pattern we seek," cried the voices, echoing again and again.

Kris reached out to touch the braid, but it was fading, vanishing into the horizon.

"Maker," said the voices.

The scene melted, replaced by a wide red desert with rocks strewn in all directions. There were three lights in the sky, forming a vertical line. The sun was setting behind distant hills, sending streaks of ruby and sapphire through the sky.

Kris bent over and picked up a handful of sand. It was reddish and shiny, rough in her hand like bits of glass.

She woke with a gasp in the darkness. Kris reached for her stainless-steel water bottle, which was cool to the touch.

"This is ridiculous. I've got to know more. Gal Pals, don't fail me now," she said to the screen, which showed four lines of text from Toor's Rix. Kris's shoulders slumped as she read them.

Widespread food shortages, lack of clean water, disease.

13.9°S 59.2°W.
Wallace factor.
Inform Four.

At best, the messages were cryptic insights into what Toor was doing. At worst, they were meaningless.

The first line was easy: the world was unraveling, which Kris already knew. The camps were overcrowded, and there wasn't enough food or water. "Disease" was a new one, however. But with people crammed together like sardines, that kind of thing was inevitable. You could catch cholera or dysentery from unclean drinking water.

Kris cracked her knuckles and entered the coordinates into Rix. There was a satellite picture of a field. She zoomed out, and there were more fields. After one more zoom-out, she found herself in western Brazil. That made no sense, unless it was Benedita's home.

"Wallace factor" was even weirder. It must be about Nate, but what did it mean? Was Toor also keeping notes on Nate, treating him like a puppet?

The last line made her head want to explode. Which four was she referring to? Four of her agents, or four of the M-Team? Kris was in that group of four mathematicians.

An idea occurred to her. She paced and held her hands to her mouth, then tried a decryption protocol. The cursor at the command prompt blinked for a whole unending minute. Then something magical happened. Toor's folders organized themselves into a ring with lines emanating from them to a central folder titled Four. Kris tapped on it and held her breath.

Inside were pictures and write-ups of everyone Kris knew, including their addresses, phone numbers, and other personal information. Nate was there, as were Sarah and Antoinette. Even her father was in there, a man she barely knew, tucked away in a trailer park in Port Alberni, British Columbia. The M-Team was there, including her. Kris shook her head; this was like watching a group of pawns in a giant chess game that Toor was playing.

There was a file on Toor too, along with ones for Diya and the other agents. The files had a hierarchy, all lines tracing back to a root folder she couldn't see. Kris typed in her meanest protocols, the nuclear ones that could decrypt anything.

Nothing emerged except for one word. All the damn lines stopped at Four.

◎ ∘ ◎

Kris knocked on the door to Antoinette's room. There was silence, so she knocked again. A beam of light hit her bare toes.

The door opened just a sliver. "It's four a.m., you weirdo. What is it?" Antoinette asked, her eyelids drooping.

Kris scanned her sister from head to toe.

Her hair was a bright platinum blond. That was odd.

She had on a Joan Jett T-shirt. That was normal.

She wore white furry bunny slippers with bright pink noses. Off the charts.

That did it. Kris laughed aloud.

"What? The slippers? Yolanda let me borrow them; my feet were freezing."

"I can't sleep," Kris said.

Antoinette rolled her eyes and opened the door. Kris sat on the edge of her bed, the sheets curled in a ball.

"Bad alien dreams again?"

Kris stared at the imperfections in the concrete floor. She didn't want to tell Antoinette about Four yet. That could wait until tomorrow.

Antoinette plopped down next to her and let out a massive yawn. Kris stared distractedly at the cute but out-of-place bunnies.

"Want to talk about it?" Antoinette asked.

Kris shook her head and pursed her lips.

"Do you remember that ancient kids' show Mom made us

watch on the old web? Before Rix was a thing. What was it called?" Antoinette asked.

"*Mister Rogers' Neighborhood*. It was so incredibly simplistic," Kris said.

"Corny is the word I would use. That show was from, like, ninety years ago. But there was one episode I remember where Mr. Rogers talked about terrible things happening, like people getting hurt. Do you remember that one?"

Kris shook her head.

"He said to look for the helpers. That when terrible things happen, there will always be people helping. Instead of focusing on the bad parts, focus on the helpers."

Kris stared right at Antoinette.

"That's what you're doing now. You're a helper," Antoinette said.

"Can I sleep here?"

Antoinette yawned again. "Yeah, okay. Get your pillow. And if you snore, I'll kick you. Do you want to hear a song I'm working on? I only have a few lines so far."

"Sure." Kris rested beside her sister.

Antoinette sang in muted tones like the song was a lullaby. Kris closed her eyes and cuddled into her pillow as her sister sang. She sighed and let the tension go from her shoulders. Soft music weaved through her mind, similar to her math music. With each line, she drifted closer and closer to slumber.

Freezing and falling,
fragrant and blue,
candles and tallow,
someone like you.
Resting and waking,
someone somewhere,
swam and shone and swooned.

CHAPTER 8

EUREKA

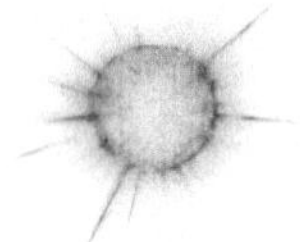

"WHAT DO YOU mean, math is beautiful?" Yolanda asked.

Kris munched her cereal. She coughed as a small piece of cornflake caught in the back of her throat, then blotted oat milk from the corner of her mouth. Antoinette had finished her breakfast, while Yolanda just had a cup of black coffee going cold in front of her. This wasn't Kris's idea of a typical Saturday morning.

"A Chanel dress is beautiful. A sunny day on a white sandy beach is beautiful. The *Mona Lisa* is beautiful. Math equations are *not* beautiful," Yolanda proclaimed, and folded her arms.

"Uh-oh. You've walked into one of Kris's math traps," Antoinette said, tossing a lock of dyed hair over her shoulder. Kris wasn't used to the new look.

"Just because *you* can't see the beauty in something doesn't mean it's not there," Kris told Yolanda.

"Damn this phone—I can't get on Rix this morning. Okay, Einstein, gimme an example. One I can understand," Yolanda said. Antoinette eyed her.

Kris paused. She wasn't sure she could explain anything without using technical terms Yolanda wouldn't understand. Antoinette mouthed, "Einstein."

"How about Euler's thingy? The one with *e* and pi," Antoinette suggested.

"Oh, good one. It's called Euler's identity," Kris said. She took a pen out of her pocket and wrote on a napkin: $e^{i\pi}+1=0$.

Yolanda was unimpressed, so Kris explained. "This simple equation is the prettiest one in mathematics. It ties together the most important numbers. There's pi, of course. Here, *e* is the natural logarithm constant, the letter *i* stands for the complex constant, and zero and one are the multiplicative and additive units—"

"Oh my god! My cell phone is working again!" Yolanda exclaimed and left the table, already typing.

Kris frowned, wondering why she even bothered.

"She can't understand the math gig, K," Antoinette said.

"Mathematics will never go out of fashion," she said.

"And it's the one way we have to get Sarah back."

Kris was unaccustomed to working on a clock. She'd viewed her mathematical research up to that point as fun, not work. After all, how could one complete a doctorate at age sixteen without seeing it as a game? Even when she'd discovered the proof of the Riemann hypothesis, it had been more like play than hard work.

But this was different. At times, it felt like the white walls of the M-Team's workroom were closing in on her. Each member of the team was a leader, all of them proven academics. And they were working in tandem with secondary and tertiary teams in undisclosed locations rife with every kind of mathematician, computer scientist, and linguist. The M-Team had the mathematical superstars, the ones humanity was counting on to end this nightmare, but they were far from the only ones involved. And among so many great *adult* minds, Kris was the outsider.

She doodled a calculation in her diary. It was a stubborn elliptic integral of the second kind. She was doing it wrong; her fingers wouldn't stay still. This kind of math was usually easy for her.

Nate bickered with Kris over the smallest things now, and working with the other mathematicians was like herding cats. This time, though, their work was about more than his reputation or another award to put on his desk. There was no academic gold star waiting at the end of this equation.

Kris made a mistake in the fourth line of the calculation. She tore the page out and crumpled it into a ball. It was wrong.

She turned her attention back to the orb in New York City. The equation she'd written in her diary just after the encounter—what did it mean?

There was nothing left but the message itself, still indecipherable. They'd thrown every theory humanity knew at it, hoping that something would stick. Kris had been racking her brain for days for something she had missed, a flaw in the message's armor. But while they'd cracked a bit of the message, they hadn't gotten past the galactic greeting. Each day of work was longer than the last.

Kris wiped sweat from her brow in the air-conditioned workspace like she was coming down with something. Toor wandered through the halls of the base, occasionally stopping at the door. She always had the same cold demeanor. She said nothing and revealed less.

Kris began the calculation of the integral again. Her pen ran out of ink, and she threw it on the floor. This time, she made even more mistakes. What was she missing? She dropped her head forward into her hands.

The gloom felt heavier than usual that day. Even Yolanda was dimmer, her usual sparkle dulled. Antoinette didn't say anything, but her smile looked phony, like she was holding it together for Kris. Whenever Kris crossed paths with them on break, the conversation fizzled into awkward silence. In the mess hall, Ari glanced at her, then looked away. He was following Toor's orders. He wasn't talking to her.

She tore another page from her diary, then flung the book against the wall.

It's not anyone else's fault that I'm too stupid to solve this math problem. I've gotta get outside, Kris thought. She picked up the diary, although the sight of it made her wither. The thing weighed a million pounds in her tiny hands.

Kris wandered to the open courtyard at the entrance to the base. Private Dax followed her like her shadow. She found Antoinette sitting outside in the sunlight, reading a book the old-fashioned way—on paper. She hated reading on her phone and enjoyed the sense of progression as she turned the pages one by one. This book, a gift from their grandmother, was one Antoinette read many times. It was one of the sentimental items she'd packed before they'd left their home. There were small beads of sweat on her brow.

"What're you doing here?" Kris asked.

"Catching a few rays. I hate the sun, but I figure if the world is ending, I should get some color before it happens."

Kris managed a half smile. She sat in the chair next to her sister and let out a slow breath.

"Do you think they would let us go home if I asked Agent Toor?"

"I doubt it. They'd send us to a camp like everyone else. Why go home now? Mom's lost in space, and the message is still a mystery."

Kris grimaced. "I don't think I can do this," she said. "The problem's too complex. It's been almost a week, and we are all stumped."

"If any human being can solve it, that freak would be you."

"We don't have enough time. Did you see the news this morning? Half the world is stuck in refugee camps with no food or water, and the other half is just fighting each other. And there are more orbs showing up everywhere. It's getting worse. I can't even watch the videos anymore without feeling sick and having to look away." Anxiety and fear began to overwhelm her like water spilling over a dam.

Antoinette took her time before responding, watching Kris shrewdly. "Then don't watch them," she finally said. "Focus on your mathematics. That's your superpower. You proved the Riemann hypothesis, remember? And I'm going to be your literary agent when they give you a million-dollar book deal."

"I've tried all the tricks, though. Even my trip to Times Square didn't make deciphering the message any easier," Kris said.

"Tell me what you've figured out so far."

"You don't like it when I talk about math."

"This time is special. So long as you don't endlessly talk about n or k." Antoinette winked, giving her a good-natured smirk.

They pulled their chairs into the shade, and Kris let the story of the M-Team's discoveries unwind. Their expertise in abstract algebra, geometry, and topology revealed only a fragment of the message's structure. The deeper parts stayed hidden. Antoinette endured the technical terms with infinite patience.

When Kris finished her explanation, Antoinette said, "Wow, I got exactly *none* of that. After my gap year, I'm going to art school, remember? Math was never my thing."

"And that's the short version," Kris said. "We're stuck. We keep going in circles, and every time we think we've got something, it falls apart. We can't think of anything else to try."

"But you guys are all looking at it as *human* math, right? What if it's *alien* math?"

Kris was silent, not sure where the conversation was going.

"You said it yourself. The aliens can have eight fingers and toes, or maybe none at all. Gross. Anyway, their way of looking at the world may—must—be different from ours. They're clearly incredibly smart if they can drop these orbs on our planet from nowhere."

Kris became still. She closed her eyes and retreated to a safe mental place, a place where she could think.

Antoinette kept talking. "You're playing the same notes. Try something weird. In music, when things get boring, someone tries something new."

Kris stayed quiet, so her sister went on. "Can you look at it another way? The aliens aren't thinking like us. They probably see more. Try to think the way they would."

"We've tried everything we know, though," Kris said.

Kris's heart fluttered as inspiration landed in her mind like a butterfly on a twig.

"*Riemann*," she whispered. "It must be the key."

"I don't follow," Antoinette said.

"We've tried everything we know," Kris said. "So maybe we need something we don't understand yet. And the biggest math mystery there is is the Riemann hypothesis."

She took a breath. "I think I've found a proof. I showed it to Nate, but even he can't totally make sense of it yet. He made me promise not to tell anyone because he's sure there's a mistake somewhere. Right now he's focused on decoding the message with the equation I wrote in Times Square. But I keep thinking Riemann might be the key."

Kris jumped to her feet, ready to go.

"Wait, it's been bugging me. You've explained it before, but what *is* the Riemann hypothesis?"

"It's about proving the real parts of the nontrivial zeroes of the zeta function lie on the critical line $z=1/2$."

"Try to explain it in English."

"You remember prime numbers, right?"

"Numbers that can only be divided evenly by one and themselves. Like two, three, and five."

"Yeah. We don't understand the *shape* of the primes. The patterns that they show up in are mysterious."

"Okay, I'm going to regret this, but go on," Antoinette said, leaning forward.

"Imagine standing in the middle of a huge forest. Every number is a tree. They spiral out from you, like rings. Most of the trees are green. The primes are red."

She paused, then continued. "If someone flew over the forest, they'd see red trees scattered everywhere. Not random. Just not obvious. The Riemann hypothesis is about understanding that pattern. It's a big problem in math. Like, really big."

"I kind of get it. Maybe. But wait a minute—why haven't you tried to apply the Riemann hypothesis to the alien message already?"

"Because I didn't trust myself enough to try it without Nate. And you made me realize that was wrong. You're kind of incredible!"

Kris kissed her sister on the cheek and ran toward the workroom. Antoinette might have saved the world.

Writing as fast as she could, Kris filled at least a half dozen boards with her proof before the rest of the team returned from their break. In her head, the familiar music of math played.

"Kris, what the hell are you doing?" Nate asked as he entered, his hands in his pockets.

"We've been approaching this from the wrong angle," she said, breathless. "Well, not the wrong one, per se, but not the right one either. Oh, I'm not good at explaining this. We've tried everything we know, right? Now it's time for the unknown. Our *greatest* unknown."

Nate figured it out after a few seconds, the idea dawning on his face like a sunrise. "Your proof of the Riemann hypothesis. Yes, of course. But wait, it wasn't ready." He crossed his arms.

The other mathematicians entered quietly. A few stopped cold in their tracks. Proving the hypothesis was no small feat. No one knew about her proof other than Antoinette and Nate.

Luke leaned back. "Once you wander this close to Riemann, something is supposed to fail, so forgive me if I'm skeptical on more than one level."

"Nate, just give me the team's attention for one hour. I can explain my proof. I know there's something in there that could help us decode the message."

Speaking rapidly, gesturing to board after board, Kris walked the team through her work. Luke, the best equipped to follow Kris's proof, gasped about halfway through. She didn't blame him. The scope of the idea was overwhelming.

When Kris finished, she waited for someone to have a reaction—any reaction. But there was silence. Kris desperately wanted them to understand. They *had* to understand.

"You lost me in the first twenty minutes, so don't expect me to start clapping," said Benedita.

Luke pulled up the three-dimensional plot Kris had discovered in the orb's message, illustrating the mirror symmetries. He overlaid the complex plane and embedded the message on a Riemann surface.

"Holy shit," Luke said.

"There! Around the critical line! *Que bonito!*" Nate screamed, jumping out of his chair.

The others stood as well. As they watched, the message began to siphon off into smaller pieces, expanding into complex patterns that overwhelmed the screen.

"It's so beautiful," Kris said.

The members of the M-Team stood speechless, looking at the dizzying patterns in awe, as if a giant veil had lifted. They saw the raw engines of the universe pulsing before them.

"It's like the message is alive," Luke whispered.

"Can we say *eureka* yet?" Kris asked.

"This is the future, right now," Benedita said, shaking her head.

"This'll take time to compile. I'll let the secondary and tertiary teams know right away," Nate said.

Kris covered her mouth and leaned against the wall for support. She wanted to cry with happiness. She braced herself as the world went sideways. They'd been waiting for this breakthrough. Finally, they'd begun to break the alien code.

◎ ◦ ◎

Kris invited Antoinette and Yolanda to her quarters, which had papers full of mathematical formulas and proofs scattered everywhere. She was relieved to have good news to share. She took some deep breaths and tried to stay calm. She failed.

"Guys, I'm losing it," she shouted as they came in. "We're cracking the message."

Kris grabbed the stack of notes and sent them flying. Antoinette froze in the doorway. She shook her head, amazed.

"This is happening? For real? Congrats! I knew you could do it," Antoinette said.

"We're deciphering the blueprint of the message. Responding will be a lot harder."

"But you're making real progress?" Yolanda said.

"Yes!" Kris had goose bumps.

"That's the best news I've heard in ages," Antoinette said.

"We should have the message deciphered in a day or so. It means no sleep for me for, like...ever, though."

Kris pictured the M-Team and their endless work, each of them having left friends and family behind. Many of them were far from home. At least she had her sister.

"We'll finally get Mom back," Kris said.

Antoinette's face softened, and she picked up one of the pieces of paper.

"I know we don't always get along," she said. "But I want you to know that I'm proud of you. I can't understand any of this, but if anyone can, it's you."

"Do you think so? I'm just a sixteen-year-old freak, remember?"

Yolanda batted her long eyelashes. She walked up to Kris and kissed her on the cheek.

"News flash, Einstein. We're all freaks, every one of us. Me, your sis, you, and the billions of other chicklets out there. Never forget that," Yolanda said.

Antoinette leaned in. "Why does she always sound like she's accidentally giving life advice?"

"I need to get back to my calculations, or Nate's head will explode," Kris said.

Antoinette winked and left with Yolanda.

Kris put her pen down, slumping ungracefully in her chair. She wiped her eyes with her hands. Being smart wasn't so bad after all. If she deciphered the message, people would love her the way they loved Yolanda.

Late that night, after another session with the M-Team, Kris found Antoinette again. This time, the two were alone. They walked as far as their security clearance permitted them to go down the road that led to the complex. The base was quiet in the evening, and the air outside was humid.

"Do you miss Mom?" Kris asked.

"Yeah. All the time. I'd give anything to get one more of her disapproving looks."

Private Dax, their chaperone, followed them discreetly, kicking up dust with his boots. Kris was never alone unless sleeping anymore, not even for a second. At least Dax stayed a respectful distance behind them.

"So now that you're finished with your little math problems, you finally have time to talk to me again?" Antoinette teased.

"What?" Kris asked.

Antoinette's mouth twitched, like she couldn't decide whether to smile. "Yeah. I'm starting to wonder if they're the reason we're even here." She looked away for a second, her shoulders tightening.

"Don't be weird about it. You were happy for me a minute ago.

I can't keep thinking about everything falling apart. I try to push it away, but it keeps coming back. Half the time this doesn't even feel real."

"More like a friggin' nightmare," Antoinette said. She stopped and faced Kris, then reached out and held her hands. "I've got to get this off my chest," she said. Her face was serious, and her hands shook. Kris recognized the look, and her stomach dropped.

"Ever since New York City, you've known Mom is alive. You've even seen her in your visions or whatever, right?"

"Yeah, in the aliens' home, where they took me."

"*Culpable.* You know, that's an interesting word. Culpable. Like when some guy snatches an old lady's purse and the person standing beside her does nothing."

"I don't know what you're talking about." Kris's hands slipped from Antoinette's.

"The person watching may not feel responsible. But they didn't yell, didn't do anything. They just watched. They're culpable. *Like you.*"

Her words were like a slap. "Not fair," Kris said.

"You're the smartest person I've ever met. And I'm pissed off at you right now because I finally figured it out. *You* caused all this—your proof of Riemann or whatever. That's the reason the orbs came!"

Kris couldn't say anything. She was frozen. Multiple feelings bubbled up inside her, and she wanted to analyze each of them, break them down and understand them before going forward.

"Maybe my proof of the Riemann hypothesis had something to do with the aliens showing up. I don't know. There's no way to be sure. It's complicated."

The moon slipped in and out of the clouds, like a hand passing slowly over a lamp, dimming the stars before lifting away. Antoinette walked a few steps and folded her arms. Private Dax looked away and whistled quietly.

"It's not complicated at all," Antoinette said.

Kris looked up and saw Orion through the clouds, a brief spot of familiarity against a rich tapestry of stars. She wanted to change the subject. "Look at them all. One of those lights out there is the home of the aliens."

Antoinette didn't respond. She looked down at the ground, defeated. "Your head is always in the clouds. You never focus on practical stuff. I'm getting tired. Tired of being treated like your sidekick."

"You're not. That's not true. You're more than that."

"Am I, though? I'm the one you turn to when you're stuck on a proof or when you fight with Sarah. What about *me*? What about what I want to do with my life? Do you have any idea how difficult it is to be your sister?"

"You think I'm the problem? You've always been jealous. You hate how things just work for me. And yeah, I know I'm gifted. You hate that." She heard herself say it and wished she hadn't. She froze.

"We both know you're Mom's favorite," Antoinette said. "Now she's lost, and maybe you caused it all with your proof."

"I'm sorry. I didn't...I didn't mean what I just said." Kris searched desperately for the right words.

Antoinette stormed off, leaving Kris alone with Private Dax.

I'm such a coward. I can't even tell my sister my real feelings—that I love her. What's wrong with me? Kris thought.

A chill sweat clung to her skin, and the ache ran deep. She scurried to her room, grabbed her diary and pored over her calculations, using her pen to follow them line by line. Sadness welled up in her. What if Mom never ever came back? A single tear dropped onto the page.

It was Sunday morning, almost one week since the orbs had appeared, and Kris hadn't seen Antoinette since their fight the night before. She was worried. She considered calling her but stopped herself. She had rehearsed a dozen ways to say she was sorry, but they all sounded phony. Distracted as she left the workroom, she bumped into Yolanda, who was holding Cindi.

"Have you seen Antoinette? I can't find her," Kris asked.

Yolanda's polished look stunned Kris. Her hair was curled, and her makeup was perfect. Cindi wagged her tail and let out a loud bark.

"No, the last time I saw her was in your room. You okay?"

"Yeah, but I need to talk to her badly."

Yolanda was silent. A cloud passed over her face, dampening the light in her eyes. Kris's throat tightened. "What's wrong?" she asked.

"Nothing. Talking about your sister made me think of my brother, who's in one of the camps outside Los Angeles," Yolanda said.

"I assumed your family was safe on a base like this."

"Yeah, I figured that too, but he didn't want special treatment. He said having a general for a dad and a famous sister didn't make him better than anyone else."

"I'm so sorry."

"That's why I was so excited to hear your news. Doesn't it mean this will all be over soon?"

For the first time, Yolanda's face betrayed tension and fear. Behind the glitter and glamor, she was as scared as everyone else. Putting on a brave face was familiar to Kris.

"We have five supercomputers working on deciphering the message. AI quantum algorithms and conceptual breakthroughs are speeding up the process, using the proof of the Riemann hypothesis. I'm certain we'll have good news soon."

Yolanda reached over to touch Kris's hand. "I hope so. For all our sakes."

"If you see Antoinette, tell her I want to talk with her," Kris said.

"Doc Kris," Ari called out. He walked up and leaned against

the wall with one hand. He had on a bright white shirt and blue shorts and open-toed black sandals.

"Heya. This order from your mom isn't fair. I've wanted to talk to you since we came back from Times Square," Kris said, glancing at Private Dax.

"I know, right? Can we talk alone, like, outside?" He exuded tension that was razor-sharp. She could see it in his eyes, which were framed with dark circles.

"Toor said you weren't supposed to talk to me. But I'll go if you don't mind Dax being there. You know he'll tell her what we say."

Ari gave a small nod, and the soldier followed them in silence.

The door opened to a wave of intense heat and sunlight, which made Kris squint. Private Dax lingered behind them as they talked near the metal doorway. Kris couldn't put her finger on it, but something was off with Ari. He looked like a caged tiger, ready to leap out of his skin.

"I know that Mom said you're off-limits, but I don't care anymore," he said.

Kris's stomach was full of butterflies. He touched her right hand, and the contact was like live electric wires. Ari was beautiful, like cool rain after a scorching summer day. His sharp brown eyes reminded her of Toor's, but his face was kinder and less secretive. She couldn't deny her physical attraction to him. Kris looked away, afraid he might see exactly how much he affected her.

"Something is bugging me. I need to know what you saw when you touched the orb. For real this time—no lies," he said. The intensity in his face made her pull her hand away and step back.

"I told you everything I remember back in your mom's office," Kris said.

"I had another dream last night, and this one was more freaky than usual. Remember how things went haywire in Times Square and time stopped? I think *I'm* the maker after all."

The heat made Kris sweat. She pulled her hair back and wiped her damp palms on her jeans. "But look at what happened when you touched the orb. It threw you backward, clear across the street."

He didn't appear to be listening.

"In my dream, I saw a whole fleet of orbs floating in the sky. They were trying to talk, but I didn't understand anything. If I went back to Times Square, I could try again with your help."

"Ari, I'm worried about you. You look like you haven't slept. And I can't do this right now. I have to see Nate and get back to work."

Kris reached for the door handle, but Ari positioned himself in front of her. Kris grimaced.

"You've gotta tell me what you saw in the nexus. The truth this time. There's some weird thing going on between you and me and the aliens. The dreams and stuff."

"Yeah, maybe. I don't really understand the dreams or any of it. There are way more questions than answers. But I have to go or Nate's going to be pissed."

She glared at him, then swung open the door, half expecting him to block her again. At least Dax was nearby, and that reassured her. Ari was acting so strangely. She couldn't deny a pull toward him like the intense gravity of a neutron star. Their mutual attraction, however, made life more complicated. If only they could have met under more normal circumstances.

"You can't run from this. You can't keep running forever," he muttered as the door closed behind her.

CHAPTER 9

THE INFINITE MESSAGE

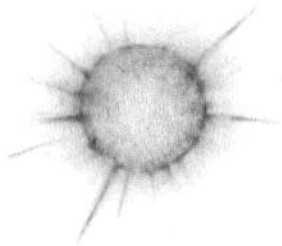

KRIS DRAGGED HERSELF to the workroom. Her anxiety and lack of sleep clawed at her insides. Antoinette wasn't speaking to her, and her feelings for Ari made her head whirl. The alien message was like a deep, impenetrable fortress, complete with a moat and a drawbridge. They'd marched through one entrance only to find the next door blocked.

Nate had called the M-Team together for another marathon session. The computing cluster with nodes all over the planet had revealed something unexpected. He stood rigid while the M-Team sat around him. He loved drama.

Nate cleared his throat and crossed his arms. "We've been studying the alien message as a team since Tuesday. Using Kris's proof of the Riemann hypothesis, we've made significant progress. But there is a major problem. We don't have enough memory to hold it in our computers."

What?

The pronouncement floored Kris. The cluster could store petabytes of information and run calculations at mind-bending speeds. Storage had never been an issue.

"How's it even possible to run out of computing space in 2035?" Luke said.

Nate let out a sigh. "For lack of a better way to phrase it, the message is infinite. It contains limitless complexity."

The word *infinite* stuck out. Kris felt it in her chest before she could make sense of it. This wasn't the kind of infinity mathematicians wrote papers about and debated over coffee. It felt physical, like diving into an ocean or standing at the base of a mountain. For the first time, she wondered whether communication with the aliens could ever happen on anything resembling equal terms.

"But there are a finite number of electrons in the universe. What you're saying makes no sense," Kris said.

"I agree, as do our top computing experts. It doesn't make any sense. And yet, there seems to be no limit to the size of the message. But I also have good news to share. What we've deciphered so far seems to be a sort of *quiz*."

Kris had no words. But in a way, it made an odd type of sense. The aliens were testing them, as she'd suspected all along.

Nate pulled up some images on the screen. It was the three-dimensional map of the message that they'd found days earlier, but now there were intricate geometric patterns highlighted in red. He zoomed in on them one by one; each contained specific mathematical concepts ranging from ordinary arithmetic to complex dynamics and beyond.

One of them referenced the Riemann hypothesis.

"Incredible!" Luke said. "It's like a kind of galactic mathematical crossword."

"The next step is for us to respond to the quiz. That's phase two of our work. While the message is infinite, we have to try to work with the parts we understand and communicate before the situation in the camps becomes even more critical."

Nate pulled up a real-time video of Times Square. Workers were building a large spherical structure around the orb. It had no top and consisted of curved walls paralleling the orb's geometry. There were large vertical slices in the dome where people could enter. The structure was in its most basic form, however, looking largely unfinished.

"This is our means of communicating with the aliens. It'll be ready in two days. Folks, we're all going to Times Square."

Fear swirled in the pit of Kris's stomach. How would the aliens react? These orbs were responsible for the disappearance of millions. One communication mishap, and who knew what would happen?

"The semispherical wall we're building is a screen. The team will input the solutions to the questions embedded in the message one by one, so they display on the screen."

"That seems odd. Why bother doing it in person? We could record the solutions and send them to the screen remotely," Benedita said.

"Agent Toor is insisting on our physical presence. She has her orders. The aliens will want to see us instead of just reading answers carved on a cave wall, as it were."

"Orders from who? You've never explained who Toor is working for," Kris asked.

Nate said nothing, and Kris's stomach tightened. She knew this was something to do with Four. Maybe Nate wasn't allowed to talk about it. She'd have to confront Toor soon to get answers.

This was her second chance to get Mom back. Maybe the last one. If she told Antoinette about it, maybe she'd talk to her again. The orbs hadn't been hostile since the incidents in Toronto and New York, no doubt because of the evacuations. No one was there to antagonize the alien artifacts. They hovered in silence.

Night descended as slowly as a sloth while Kris worked with the M-Team on the final preparations. That evening after dinner, she sat with Yolanda in the base's mess hall. It had become like their second home.

"We're going to visit the orb, try to talk to it again," Kris said to break the silence.

"That sounds dangerous. I don't want to be anywhere near that thing," Yolanda said.

"I was already near it, and I didn't vanish," Kris said.

"Why do you have to be there? Couldn't you have a computer relay the message you want to send?"

Kris pushed her plate forward. "They want *us* there. Toor's superiors gave the orders. We need to be able to communicate with the aliens on their terms. That's the test."

Humanity had many destructive tendencies, even self-destructive ones. It was possible the aliens were giving them a chance to prove they could produce something beyond all of that. Like a test of worthiness before they were invited into the cosmic club.

"If everyone else is going, then can I come? Please? I hate that thing, but I'd feel safer with you and Toor and the others around. My father will be there too," Yolanda said.

"It's not my call. You'll have to ask Toor. Have you seen Antoinette?" Kris asked, her chest tight.

Antoinette was nowhere to be found, and she was the sole person Kris trusted there on the base. Their fight, still fresh in her mind, made her cringe. They'd each said horrible things. She'd never spoken that way to her older sister before. And their fight had come from nowhere.

Kris tried to sleep that night but couldn't. She closed her eyes. She could see the orbs flashing and she could see Sarah. Her fight with Antoinette haunted her. *Was* she responsible for what was happening with the orbs? She wasn't sure. Thinking about mathematics stressed her out way more than usual. At one a.m., she stopped struggling and opened a screen to view the progress of the cluster. Her screen filled with plots and formulas. Something had been clawing at her subconscious, trying to break through, but the idea made no sense.

Nate had said that the message was *infinite*. He was confident on that point, no matter how strange it sounded. It was a widely debated philosophical question: Was the universe finite or infinite? Most people assumed it must be finite. Humans knew the size of the universe; they knew how much matter it contained. There was a limit to it all, like the population of a city or the number of grains of sand on a beach. The number was large, unthinkably vast, but it could only get *so* big.

But those were human-defined limits. It was clear now that they saw only a fraction of the universe, like they saw a fraction of the electromagnetic spectrum in the form of visible light. There were mathematical patterns everywhere in nature, from black holes to the flight of bumblebees. Why couldn't there be patterns permeating the fabric of reality as well?

It made Kris's head spin. She sat up, scratched her back, and grabbed her diary. It was cool in her hands. Reassuring.

Monday, July 23, 2035, she wrote. *If the human race survives this, we need to change how we look at the universe, how we look at ourselves. First, we know now that we're not alone. We also know that the aliens are more advanced than we are. Our quest for deeper understanding is now limitless. With near infinite knowledge, who knows what the aliens are capable of?*

Why is Ant mad at me when I need her most?

Inspiration struck, but the late hour caused her to pause. She needed to consult the resident experts, the other members of the M-Team. As Erdős used to say, a mathematician's brain was often open, regardless of the hour. Kris called Lara Armistead, the Parisian who was the top expert in geometry on the M-Team. Lara was half asleep as she stared, zombielike.

"Sorry to disturb you, but I have an idea about the alien message, and I need to talk to you."

The woman eyed Kris warily through the screen.

"Infinite-dimensional topology. Can you share what you know?"

"*Merde.* You woke me up at this hour to talk about that? Should I be insulted or flattered? Or both?" Lara asked in her French accent.

"Flattered. I could scan through your many books, but why bother when you, the world's leading expert, are here in the flesh? Would you please come to the workroom? I need to talk to you right now."

Lara's eyelashes fluttered, and she inclined her head a fraction. The screen went blank.

They met in the workroom, Lara holding a cup of coffee and an unlit cigarette. They were legal in France, but not here. "Nathaniel will be pissed if I smoke in here, but how do you say in English? I don't give a shit?" she said, throwing her knapsack on a chair.

"Please, Lara. I need your help."

Lara approached the board. She lit her cigarette and took three long drags. She threw her half-smoked cigarette into her coffee cup; it sizzled as it hit the liquid. After a brief silence, Lara began to write. Kris stood back and watched, forcing herself to ignore the strong odor of the smoke. She tried not to choke.

What followed blew Kris's mind. She'd never worked in this field before. Much of her intuition failed when it came to infinite dimensions, as the subject relied on analytic foundations rather than standard geometry.

"Kris, why the sudden interest in my theories? You work in combinatorics and number theory, not infinite-dimensional topology."

"The many-worlds theory in theoretical physics," Kris replied.

Despite all the conjecture, no one had ever proved it. Physicists had toyed with the idea for decades, and recent theories used the idea of an infinite set of universes all occupying adjacent space in an infinite-dimensional manifold. There was no experimental evidence for it, though. Scientists weren't sure how to devise an experiment to find the hidden dimensions.

Still, the idea of infinitely many parallel universes was plausible. For example, there were some in which Kris had tea instead of coffee after dinner. Some in which she hadn't called Lara. Some in which she'd just moved her hand to the left instead of the right. Each moment was rife with endless possibilities. What if they existed, every possibility, irrevocably recorded in the multiverse but out of reach?

"The message is *infinite*, like Nate said. And I think we've been looking at it the wrong way. We kept treating it like it was finite, like something with an end. But that doesn't work. That's why we can only understand pieces of it."

"If the alien message is infinite and the universe is finite…" said Lara. She looked like lightning had struck. She leaned forward. "Yes! Yes, I see where you're going with that idea. If the aliens can access hidden dimensions, then they could store their data there. Each pocket universe would contain a finite amount of data, but taken as a whole, there would be an infinite amount. Hold on. We're talking about something akin to dimensional engineering. This is absurd."

"Don't they have *Doctor Who* in Paris?" Kris asked. "The TARDIS is bigger on the inside than the outside. It's kind of like that. The aliens built their own version, except it's a computer."

"It wouldn't even need to be an infinite number of dimensions. If they could parallelize computation in even a few thousand dimensions, then the speed and storage capacity would be greater than anything we can conceive. Throw in quantum computing, and it could explain how these aliens weave their magic."

"Could you even build a model of computation in infinite dimensions? In theory?"

"Hmmm. I suppose so, in theory. It would never have any practical use, though, so long as these dimensions remain inaccessible to us."

"But you could do it?" Kris asked.

"Hold on a second. We need this first."

She reached into her knapsack and produced a small package wrapped in foil. She peeled the foil back, and Kris almost fell off her chair.

"Oh...my...god! Is that what I think it is?"

Lara gave an impish grin. "*Oui*. Eighty-five percent dark chocolate. Real Belgian stuff. The official food group of higher mathematics."

The morning hit, and Kris knew she would always remember that day. She and Lara had worked through the night, trying to create a rough draft for a working theoretical model of the aliens' multi-dimensional computer.

"I have doubts. I don't see how this precisely will help us. It's not a practical design. We exploited ideas from geometry and topology to show how it *could* work, but—how do they say it in your Quebec? *Tabernac*," said Lara.

"We don't need to build it. We just need a *model*. If it's right, the message should start to come together in ways we can actually work with. And we need that. If we mess up their quiz, who knows what happens."

"*Oui, oui*, but we are missing the optimal transport equations. Those will tell the system how to move the information across dimensions. Otherwise, it will not work."

Kris almost fell out of her chair. *Of course—the equations I wrote out in Times Square!* She could see how it all connected. She brought up the equations, and Lara's eyes looked like they would pop out. Kris could make out a faint thread of music stirring in the background, and she knew she was on to something.

"Yes! Those nonsensical equations that you and Nate shared with the M-Team. I stared at those pesky little creatures for hours to no avail. However, if we transform the variables using our algorithms, then these could be exactly what we need," Lara said.

"Look at this," Kris said.

Kris entered her equations. Without hesitation, Lara input a program for the circuits of their virtual computer.

"Here goes nothing," Kris said, tapping the enter key.

Lara lit another cigarette, and Kris resisted the urge to cough. The two of them sat silently, focused on the screen. It displayed an intricate flow diagram, pumping information from one side to the other. Lara tapped her controls, and the diagram expanded into three dimensions, revealing an algorithm working at a level of complexity Kris hadn't dreamed was possible. Time froze as they tested the new virtual computer, entering bits of the orb's message into it.

Right at eight a.m., the rest of the M-Team converged on the workroom. Nate entered and paused as he looked at the screens, which were full of complex mathematical expressions.

"What's all this? And what's that smell? Lara, were you smoking in the workroom again?" he asked.

Lara and Kris locked eyes, deadly serious. Then Kris burst into laughter. Lara let out her signature raspy cackle. To Kris, she was the coolest person in the world just then.

"For the record," Kris said, "we were not running on coffee, chocolate, or anything else."

Nate glanced at the empty coffee cups, then let out a thin breath.

"Monsieur Wallace, we designed the world's first logically consistent infinite-dimensional computer," said Lara. She coughed and hid her coffee cup, which served as an ashtray, below her desk.

Lara and Kris explained their ideas to Nate and the M-Team. Something in his expression shifted, like a lock clicking open.

"Of course! Once intelligence computes across neighboring dimensions, the machine isn't the substrate anymore. The universe is," he said. Even Kris didn't follow all of it, but she saw the recognition in his eyes.

The concepts they presented were weird. They were talking about a working infinite-dimensional computer, after all, at least theoretically. Quantum computers had existed on paper long before they worked in the real world. In principle, why couldn't their theory work the same way? They were building the next wave of computers, which would make those seem like pocket calculators by comparison.

"The optimal transport equations are the ones Kris brought back from her visit to the orb," Lara said. "The ones we were all stuck on. They are the oil for the engine, as it were."

"Here goes nothing," Nate said as he entered the orb's message into the theoretical computer model. He tapped on the screen. His command activated the advanced computing cluster of the tertiary team.

Time inched by. The program littered the screen with indecipherable code, never pausing, never stopping. The tension was thick. Kris had to remind herself to breathe.

Abruptly, the program stopped and output a file. What emerged startled every member of the M-Team. Kris's head hummed with excitement or fatigue—she couldn't tell which. The message was infinite, but it had resolved itself into manageable parts, neatly arranged like folders on a desktop.

She was sure the others were thinking the same thing as she was: *There's no going back.*

The message wasn't a greeting or a quiz. It was all of that, but it was also an encyclopedia containing vast stores of mathematical theory—galactic mathematics brought to them by the orb aliens. The aliens had locked much of it away, with the unlocked pieces relating to certain as-yet-unanswered questions. Perhaps humans weren't ready to see it all. At least not yet.

High fives and cheers broke out as it sank in what they'd done. The team had revealed the message in full.

"You did it! Kris, you did it! This is absolutely groundbreaking," said Nate.

Kris relished the moment. It was rare to receive sincere praise from Nate. Lara hugged Luke, and Benedita hugged Kris in triumph.

"I need to use the washroom. Back soon," Kris said.

As she walked down the hall, Kris couldn't shake the feeling that someone was following her. She stopped and looked over her shoulder. No one was there.

CHAPTER 10

BREAKING POINT

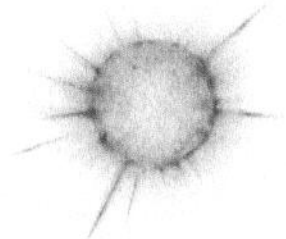

O N THE WAY back, Kris stopped in her room to double-check one of her calculations on the display by her bed. It was so much easier to think about mathematics when she was alone. She sat at her desk and scratched the top of her head. She scribbled her ideas on a piece of paper.

"We've gotta talk," Ari said in a half whisper, making her jolt.

Kris swiveled her chair to look at him standing in the doorway, his shoulders hunched and his eyes glassy.

"We already said everything we needed to say."

"Can I come in?"

"Toor said you can't speak to me. You're going to get us both in trouble. Maybe you should go." Something was off with him.

Ari entered and leaned on the wall opposite her bed. "This place is gross and dull. But Mother likes it," he said. He ran his fingers through his black hair, which fell loose around his forehead. His eyes were like hallways ending in sadness rather than hardness like Toor's. Kris put her pencil down.

"This whole thing isn't *fair*," he continued.

"What're you talking about?" asked Kris. She pushed back in her chair, and it creaked.

"Nothing's fair. The orbs talk to you but not me. You've got it easier."

Kris let out a long sigh. "For real? You have no idea what it's like to be me."

"To be the center of attention? To be a world-famous math whiz? I get it now."

"I don't want to be any of that."

"What do you want, then?"

"What you have. To have my mom back." Kris bit her lip and resisted the urge to tear up.

Ari was silent. He tipped his head back against the wall and stared at the ceiling. He mumbled something Kris couldn't make out.

"What? I can't hear you."

"It's not fair," he whispered again, his face betraying his fear and regret.

Inside, beneath his good looks, Ari was troubled. Like Kris, he clearly felt like the odd one out. He'd mentioned in New York that he'd run away from home before. He was brilliant but neglected by a parent who didn't seem to care.

Kris felt for him. She had a loving family and a stable home, but she also had her own personal prison sentence to face. She faced years of toil, working on mathematics that only a handful of experts could understand. Was that the way she wanted to live out the rest of her life? Had Nate or Sarah ever asked her if she wanted another life, one that didn't involve mathematics?

"She's ruined my life by making me move from place to place all the time. I can't ever make friends because we're never in any one place long enough. Sometimes, Mom goes away for weeks or months, and I have to stay with my grandparents in D.C. When I ask her about what she's doing, she just says, 'It's Four business.'"

Four. Kris sighed and scratched the back of her head once again.

"Listen...I get it," she said. "I never went to a regular school after the age of six. Other kids said I was too weird to play with.

I could factor six-digit numbers in my head while they struggled with simple fractions. But that doesn't mean I stopped trying to fit in or be normal."

Images popped into her brain of Antoinette taking her skating at Nathan Phillips Square when she was ten. Kris kept falling and falling. Her ankles hurt so much she cried. Antoinette made mocking faces at her and told her she was a loser. Anger motivated her to get up and try again and again and again. After hours of trying, she finally got it. She could skate, awkwardly at first, her legs stiff and uncertain as the blades rasped against the ice. Antoinette applauded and pretended to yawn. It was so tough to learn, but in the end, she'd mastered it. She'd never do a double axel, but at least she could skate like other kids.

Ari was silent. The fire in his eyes had softened. His nostrils weren't flared anymore. He looked down and sighed.

"I'm not okay. Ever since the orbs came, I've been *wrong*."

Kris walked over and put her hand on his cheek. She wanted to comfort him. His face was burning hot like he had a fever. He reached his arms around her and hugged her tight. Kris exhaled and nestled her chin into the crook of his collarbone.

They held each other, and time decelerated into slow, incremental steps.

"I know it's not fair. None of this is. But we're going to talk to the orbs. We figured something out," Kris whispered in his ear.

He let go and stepped backward, and as Ari met Kris's gaze, his eyes went from dull to lit up to hard. He grabbed her arm and squeezed hard enough that she wanted to smack him.

"Let go," she said.

"No. You did all of this. Look what you've done to the world."

"Let go!" Kris screamed.

"Let her go, or I'll rip your hand off," Antoinette said, standing in the doorway, her hands curled into fists and her face boiling red. Kris knew that look and hid from her sister whenever she wore it. Beads of cold sweat formed on Kris's temples, and she tried to yank herself free.

"Don't tell me what to do," he said, letting Kris go. She stumbled backward and cried out.

"You goddamn jerk!" Antoinette screamed, charging at him. Kris lurched back another step.

Antoinette threw a punch at his face. He ducked, and her fist missed him. She grabbed his left shoulder and tried to scratch his face with the nails of her free right hand. He grunted and pushed Antoinette on her right shoulder. She was taller than him but was no match for his strength. She lost her balance and fell backward. Antoinette's head hit the corner of the desk with a dull thud. She lay on the floor. She didn't move.

Ari locked eyes with Kris in disbelief. A small pool of blood formed at the back of Antoinette's head, staining her platinum hair a dark red.

"No! Ant!" Kris cried. She ran to her sister, dropping to her knees by her side. Kris's heart pounded. Antoinette was quiet—too quiet. "Please wake up, please wake up. Ant!"

She wasn't responding. Kris searched for a pulse in her neck but couldn't find it. Images of Antoinette flashed through her mind, memories from when she was little all the way to the present day. Tears filled her eyes.

At last, Kris felt Antoinette's pulse; it was slow but steady. Kris put her cheek to her sister's mouth and felt a small gust of warm air on her skin.

"How can this be happening? Dax! Help, quick!" she shouted.

"He's not there. I told him Mom was looking for him so we could be alone."

"What did you do?" Kris screamed, her hand on Antoinette's temple.

"I didn't...I didn't mean..." Ari mumbled, his face contorting as his eyes filled with tears. Then his eyes hardened once again, and his hands curled into menacing fists. Kris gasped.

The bathroom door flew open with a slam, revealing a shocked Yolanda.

Kris cried out. She could barely hear what Yolanda was saying.

The world was spinning. Yolanda gripped Antoinette and cried out. Images of the nexus flashed through Kris's mind, pulsing with power and light. Space melted away, and there was nothing but a buzz of patterns swirling behind her closed eyes. The white braid beamed and dazzled in the distance. Her body shook.

Then Kris opened her eyes. She was herself again. *What happened?* she thought.

Kris heard a click. Yolanda had a black handgun pointed at Ari. He lifted his hands, shaking his head in fear and panic. He stumbled backward, hitting the wall hard with his left hand. His mouth was moving; he was saying something, but Kris couldn't hear him.

"Yolanda, no!" screamed Kris.

Yolanda tightened her grip on the gun. "Stop now, or I'll hurt you. I know how to use this. My father made sure of that." Her voice wavered.

Ari grimaced, panic in his eyes. He ran.

Yolanda tossed the gun on the bed like a dirty rag and ran to Kris and Antoinette. Together, they sobbed and held each other over Antoinette's still form.

"She's breathing, but she's hurt. What do we do?" Kris asked.

"We've got to get help right now!" Yolanda said, her voice cracking.

Kris wanted to run. But there was nowhere to go. Nowhere to escape from the darkness enveloping her.

Kris sat beside Antoinette in the infirmary. The medbed's AI traced her vitals with steady columns of light, adjusting her medication on its own without a human nearby. Her sister looked like she was sleeping, peaceful. It was hard for Kris to imagine that she couldn't get up.

"I can't believe I'm alone in this place," Kris said.

The doctors had said Antoinette was in a coma. The desk had fractured her skull, and she had a traumatic brain injury. She could have died if the impact had been just a bit different. Even so, there was a chance of permanent brain injury. And while the doctors said that she could wake up, they couldn't say when. It could be hours, days, or weeks. Or never.

Ari had done this. Ari had lied to Private Dax, telling him Toor urgently wanted to see him. Ari had arranged the confrontation so that he could be alone with Kris.

Kris put her head in her hands and closed her eyes. She tried to push away the fear gnawing at her. She watched Antoinette, and pain stabbed at her chest. If Yolanda hadn't been there, hadn't had a gun in her purse, Ari could have done something worse. Kris reached for Antoinette's hands. Her sister's skin was warm to the touch.

"I'm so sorry, Ant," Kris whispered.

"I don't know if I'll get another chance to say this. Or to thank you. Or to tell you how much I love you."

She swallowed. "You were always there. Always. You held my hand in the hallway before my defense. You chased those kids away when they were awful to me. You followed me to New York even when it was dangerous."

Her voice broke. "And I never said it. I never told you how much you mattered. How much you still matter."

"And now you might not wake up. And I can't stop thinking that this is my fault."

Kris shivered, wiping her face with her sleeve. They were so different, she and Ant. She used to think that her sister was adopted. Sarah had done what she could to make them feel equally important, but Kris had always been the star.

What about Antoinette's talents, though? She wasn't a mathematician, but she was a kick-ass songwriter. She was always there for Kris when she needed her most, even if she could be bossy and grumpy. When Sarah had vanished, the two of them had grown closer than ever before.

But Kris knew Antoinette blamed her for Sarah's disappearance. After all, it was Kris's proof that had triggered the wave of orbs that led to the vanishing of millions. Kris had blood on her hands. She wanted to wipe it off. She wanted to fix every ruined thing.

She had to help her mom and Antoinette. She had to help the world by responding to the message. But she didn't think she could handle that responsibility right now. She was too lost in the hurricane of emotions swirling through her.

Kris kissed Antoinette's forehead and stroked her snow-white hair away from her face. "You're my hero."

"She believes in you," Nate said from the doorway.

Kris looked up at him and said nothing. Her chest heaved, and she wiped her wet nose with her sleeve.

"Because of who you are. Because you are one in a billion."

"I don't need a pep talk right now." She winced and dropped her head.

"At your doctoral defense, we were brutal, picking apart every equation and deduction. You stood there and walked us through your proof of the Collatz conjecture. I was half hoping that we would find an error, because I never imagined you could achieve such an incredible result. I was pigheaded. I could not have been more mistaken about you."

"The last time I saw her, we had a fight," Kris said, shaking with sobs.

Nate walked toward her and put a hand on her shoulder. It was a cold gesture. She wanted to be alone with her sister.

"I know it seems impossible. But we can make this work."

"I don't think I can do it alone. They're both gone," she said. Kris had difficulty swallowing around the lump in her throat.

"You aren't alone. I'm with you," he whispered.

Kris looked straight at him, her eyes burning. *Does he mean it? Can he help me?*

"Take as much time as you need, but come to my office when you are ready. I've got to talk to you about something important."

Antoinette was in a coma, and Nate was still on about the mission. The people Kris loved were gone. Sarah was gone, now Antoinette.

She'd imagined many times before what it would be like to be completely alone. She expected to curl into a ball and cry forever, like the day she'd lost Sarah in the mall at eight, her heart hammering so hard she could barely breathe. She'd imagined being ninety and standing in the rain at Ant's funeral, her family now just ashes and memories. But this was different. It was so cold, so dark, like a black pool enveloping her.

The tears on her face had dried. She was so cold. The world was so dark.

Kris walked to Nate's office like a zombie. She was tired, defeated.

They sat across from each other at his wide desk, which was like a canyon between them.

"We're going to go ahead with it, what Toor is asking for. The plan to talk to the orb in Times Square. I need you to help lead the team. Inspire them to help finish the task."

Kris wiped her eyes with her hands. Her body tightened up. "I don't think I know how."

"They'll follow you. The other members of the M-Team respect your brilliance. Also, Toor asked that you do it."

Kris remained silent. Nate widened his eyes expectantly. Now was the time for her to show her cards.

This bullshit has gotta stop, Kris thought. She had a theory, one crafted from clues she'd learned from Gal Pals and the orbs. She'd woven it together until the bonds were strong. She could be wrong, but there was nothing to lose at this point.

"One condition."

"What is that?"

Kris paused and swallowed. Her throat was dry, and her heart fluttered quickly.

"I want to talk to the puppet masters. Four, or whatever you call them."

Nate's mouth half opened. His eyes were grave.

"Don't act shocked. It was easy enough to hack into Toor's communications. I've been reading all of Toor's secret messages. Either I talk to them, or I'm done."

Kris was waiting in Toor's office when she arrived. Toor's eyes were hard as stone. Nate had explained earlier that Ari was isolated and under guard. Expectant silence settled over the room as they sat there with Nate. Toor's face was pale and rigid.

"I don't know what I can say. As his mother, I apologize for Ari's actions. We will provide the best care for Antoinette until she recovers. Ari is in a place where he can't touch you, I promise you that. When this is over, he will need to answer for what he's done."

Kris bit her lip. She wanted to shout at Toor, to scream every swear word she knew. Instead, she sighed.

Toor continued, "Ari has always had difficulties, but it became worse for him when the dreams about the orbs began. The orbs triggered something in him like they triggered something in you. But you have to understand, he's my *son*." The word *son* came out like she was choking on it.

Kris looked at the floor. The room descended into a murky silence.

"No more secrets," Kris finally said, breaking the silence with a hammer. "I need to talk to your bosses. Your *real* bosses."

"They want to talk to you too. They rarely grant an audience to any individual outside of Four." Toor coughed.

Kris drew deep from her inner strength once again. She needed answers.

"Believe me when I say that I'm sorry about Antoinette." Toor opened a screen on the wall adjacent to her desk. It was a split screen that showed multiple images of the orbs, all from different parts of the world. Every one was black. Silent.

"This is a live feed from every orb on the planet."

Kris lifted her hand to her mouth. Beside her, Nate went still, every part of him listening.

Toronto, New York, Beijing...all pitch-black like a moonless night.

"Why? Why did they go dark? I don't understand," Nate said.

The screen on Toor's desk flashed red. Four was calling.

"What you are about to hear is top secret. You cannot discuss what you learn here with anyone."

"This will be quite something," Nate said. Kris's eyes narrowed. Nate knew nothing about them, or at least he was pretending not to. "What should I expect? The bogeyman?"

Toor touched an icon on her tablet, and a blank white screen projected on the wall. The sound of static filled the space, and then a single voice emerged. It was impossible to categorize it or assign it a gender.

"Dr. Argentia, it's a shame we have to meet under these circumstances," the faceless voice said. It was unearthly, atonal.

"It's weird not seeing you. Any chance we can speak face-to-face?" Kris asked.

"Dr. Argentia, let's not be trivial. You requested to speak with us. We complied."

The only people Kris had met who used the word "trivial" regularly were mathematicians.

"You are Four?" she asked.

"Yes, we are called that. Four is an organization that includes Toor and the other agents." The atonal voice was unsettling.

"The name suggests there are four of you in charge, but I hear one person. You like to talk in riddles, I see. Like Agent Toor. In any case, you run this operation?" Kris said.

"I'm one of many. One of our main directives is discretion."

Kris blinked. Why was she so special to them?

"Why has no one ever heard of you?" Kris asked.

Silence. Then the voice said, "Come, now, this is not the time to address these questions. There is so little time left before the crisis becomes *critical*. The orbs have stopped streaming their message. That is bad for us. Bad for the world. We must move quickly now. The mission is to respond to the alien message and bring the abducted people home to their loved ones safely."

Kris listened hard, trying to place the voice, but it stayed unfamiliar.

"Of course, we will continue to help," Nate said, leaning back in his chair.

They needed her. She wanted to play along. For now.

"You are saying that if I cooperate, then Sarah, my mom, will return?"

There was a pause, and then, "That is our best chance of success, yes."

"Then I agree too."

"Good. The next step is to meet with the military. We'll contact Toor in twenty-four hours to hear about your progress."

"But I have questions. For example—"

The screen turned off, leaving them staring at a blank wall.

"Very good," Toor said. "We'll arrange a debrief with the agents and military commanders in two hours. Also, I'm having a dossier on the project sent to each of you. I suggest reviewing it in detail before the meeting."

"You guys are incredibly spooky—you know that, right?" Kris said. Toor said nothing.

Whoever Four were, it was a race against time now to get that response encoded and ready. This was Kris's one chance to get Sarah back.

◎ ◦ ◎

Kris closed the door and sat on the bed, pulling the tablet onto her lap. The files Toor had sent opened in lines of type, with black bars smothering whole paragraphs.

CONFIDENTIAL—FOUR/OPERATIONS

ORIGIN: [REDACTED]

LEADERSHIP: UNKNOWN

DIRECTIVES: SUPPRESSION/MOBILIZATION

Her eyes lingered on the last word: *mobilization*. It had the cold weight of inevitability. She scrolled through the reports in the dossier: intercepted transmissions, redacted memos, fragments of old intelligence briefings. No single document gave the full picture.

Kris needed answers. *Where had Four come from? Who led it?*

One page had Toor's handwriting in the margin, a note that Four was a mix of government operatives, generals, clergy, and billionaires. Even Toor didn't seem to know exactly who her bosses were. There were grainy video clips as well: footage from a fighter pilot's helmet cam, a blurred light over a field, a witness statement cut off mid-sentence. The reports on most of the files labeled them as inconclusive or likely hoaxes. The obscurity wasn't accidental. There were too many reports and too many dismissals.

Another header snapped into place:

FOUR PRIMARY MISSION:

Suppress evidence of extraterrestrial contact. Control narrative. Invalidate leaks.

Kris let out a long, measured breath. Her hands shook. The scope of the evidence was staggering. Every rumor, every scrap of UFO lore she'd half dismissed—Four had done its best to hide them. Yet not all could be hidden. The orbs were proof of that.

She scrolled further and found the second directive.

FOUR SECONDARY MISSION:

Mobilize global response.

Toor's note followed: *Unprepared for scale. Mars incident triggered activation.*

Valles Marineris. Toronto. New York. Beijing. The names lined up in Kris's head like falling dominoes. She leaned back against the headboard, and she let the tablet go. None of this gave her certainty. Four was still faceless and opaque; Toor was their pawn, but she was only one piece on a larger board.

At the end of the list of files were fragments: an unfinished report, a list of orb sightings through history, a reference to celestial spheres in ancient texts. Kris closed the tablet, but the details she'd read continued to burn bright in her mind. Her pulse quickened.

There was the orb contacting the rover on Mars. There was Four, invisible to the public. There was the top-secret history she'd only just learned. What powers did Four have? Kris shivered and tried not to imagine the worst.

She had seen the nexus where the orbs lived with her own eyes. Now she accepted that Four probably knew more about that, too, than they would ever admit.

Kris sat by Antoinette's bed and stared at the serene face of her sister.

"It took a coma to shut you up for once," she said. Her eyes stung from crying. "I'm a terrible sister for letting this happen to you."

There was so much pain. So much darkness. So little hope.

A gentle hand touched her shoulder. It was Yolanda. Before she could say anything, Yolanda asked, "Are you okay?" Her voice was quieter than usual.

"Yes, thanks to you." Her voice broke as she spoke.

"My dad asked me to keep a handgun ready during all of this. He even taught me how to use it. I never imagined...I never imagined I would have to use it like that."

Kris sighed. "They say she may wake up. But this kind of injury could leave her brain damaged. Or she might remain like this for a long time. Years, even."

Kris turned and looked at her. Tears welled in Yolanda's eyes.

"I don't know what I'll do without her," Kris said.

Tears streamed down Yolanda's cheeks like black rivers, her makeup ruined. "I know what it's like. I have a kid brother, remember?"

She stooped down and hugged Kris, their heads pressed together. Kris exhaled.

"I'm here for you. For both of you."

"Thank you. That means a lot," Kris whispered in her ear. "I've got to go. The M-Team is meeting. The orbs have stopped flashing, so we've got to move even quicker now."

"I'm going to stay with her, if that's okay?"

"Yeah, of course," Kris said. As she left, she lingered to watch Antoinette's face. It was as if she were asleep.

The M-Team gathered in the workroom, huddling around Kris and Nate as they waited for everyone to arrive. They looked shaken. Kris did her best to muster up her courage, but it was Nate who spoke to them first. *Nate saw the Four dossier, too,* she thought. If so, his calm was either a mask or something far more unsettling.

"Given that the orbs have gone dark, many governments are putting pressure on us to attempt communication. Our latest breakthroughs make this achievable, and in twenty-four hours, we will use what we've learned to respond to the orb. We have more than a dozen supercomputing clusters working around the clock, along with the secondary and tertiary teams. But we will be the ones on site at Times Square."

"Your sister, Antoinette—is she okay?" Luke asked. He stroked his long beard.

"She's in a coma. We don't know if she will recover," Nate said.

"My god, I am so sorry," said Benedita, looking at Kris with big brown eyes. She dropped her gaze after a moment.

Kris fought to remain silent. She wanted to burst out crying, but now wasn't the time. She had to hold it together. For Sarah. For Antoinette. She told herself over and over that Antoinette was asleep, only asleep. Around her, the team continued talking. Things weren't going the way she hoped. Kris had to do something or the group would fracture.

"None of that matters," she said. "What we do next does. We've decoded the message. Now we have to send something back. If we don't do it fast enough, we could end up like the others." Kris startled herself with the force of her words.

Nate spoke next. "We have hours to encode the proof of the Riemann hypothesis and about a dozen other advanced mathematical proofs into a format the aliens could understand. Our backup teams will do the translation grunt work, so our job is more high-level. We need to write the proofs in a salient form, something that can be logically encoded."

"We have to work together to solve this," Kris said.

A tense silence fell as the members of the M-Team stared at one another.

"Tell me where to begin," Benedita finally said. Benedita laced hands with Kris, warmth pulsing through her touch. "I'll follow the one who proved the Riemann hypothesis."

Kris squeezed her hands once, but there was a pain inside, stabbing at her heart. It reminded her of the others who'd trusted her—like Antoinette. She swallowed and pushed her pain down into a dark, windowless place. She wouldn't let herself feel anything until this was over, when the orbs were gone and their people were back.

"Are you on board?" Nate asked the rest of them.

They agreed. Kris sat with Benedita.

"I wanted you to know that I'm sorry about your sister. I am praying for her. We never doubted you or the mission for a second," the woman said.

Kris wiped a tear from her eye. These were the few people in the world who understood her burden, who grasped the enormous weight she carried.

◎ ∘ ◎

The M-Team took their meals in the workroom so they could focus all of their energy on their task. By eight p.m., Kris's eyes were blurry, and a break was in order. It was going to be an all-nighter.

They were so close to having the key constructs translated that she could taste it. It was amazing to her that these sophisticated systems of mathematics could be boiled down to a series of monochromatic flashes on a black background.

If we talk to them, then what? Will they talk back? Kris wondered.

No one had wondered aloud about what would happen next. Kris's hope was that the aliens would leave after returning those who were missing. But none of the M-Team knew for sure the outcome after they made contact.

Kris stopped by the mess hall around midnight. Cindi barked

when she entered, running up and putting her paws on Kris's legs. When she picked the dog up, she licked Kris's hands. She loved dogs and their unconditional love. What were orbs and mathematical messages to them?

Yolanda was uncharacteristically silent. She looked small, not her usual vivacious self. She was focused on typing something on her screen. "I'm sending out a message on Rix about you and the M-Team and what happened to Antoinette. How heroic you both are."

"Thank you, Yolanda. I mean, thank you again."

Yolanda shushed her. "How's it going?"

"OK. I mean probably OK. But we're close to encoding our message. It should be ready to go in the morning."

"That's something, at least."

"Why are you up so late?" Kris asked.

"I can't sleep. I try—I put my head on my pillow and cuddle with Cindi—but I can't," Yolanda said.

"Me neither, lately," Kris admitted. "My mind races even faster at night."

She gave Yolanda a small smile, scratched Cindi's ears, said good night, and walked back to her bedroom. She lay on her bed, staring at the blank ceiling. It was around one a.m. when exhaustion took her. As her eyes closed, she tried not to relive Antoinette's injury over and over.

Kris woke up and checked her phone: 3:07 a.m. She stopped by the workroom, where she found Nate. They were working in shifts to prepare for the communication attempt.

"You should rest," Nate said. "We have much to do, and I need your brain in top form."

"Can't. I want to work instead. Do you mind?"

"Suit yourself."

Kris opened a screen and worked for an hour. She fought back fatigue, but she was close to running out of steam. Once lost, she feared it might not come back so easily.

Her eyelids were heavy, and she closed them against the dim

light of the screen. Her head fell forward, and she woke with a start. She lay her head on her folded arms, and sleep came like a cool wave.

She was on the beach in a white dress, walking out into the ocean. The water was warm, and the white fabric spread out around her as she walked in deeper, the water now up to her waist. As she turned around to look back, a lone figure, also dressed in white, walked toward her—a young woman with black hair.

"Ant!" Kris screamed, waking up in a cold sweat. Had she killed both her sister and her mom?

CHAPTER 11
CONVERGENCE

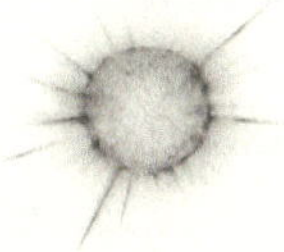

BEWILDERED, KRIS WOKE to see the workroom empty of people. Her mind was blank. Her neck and shoulders ached. She scrambled out into the hallway and heard voices coming from the mess hall. She'd been asleep in her chair for an hour.

"Nate, what's all this?" Kris asked as she entered the space where Nate, the M-Team, and Yolanda watched a screen projected on the wall. She immediately sensed the gravity of everyone's mood.

The screen said the time was six a.m. on Tuesday morning, and the breaking news feed indicated that India and Pakistan were now at war. Many hundreds of soldiers had already died in skirmishes in the border towns in Kashmir. There was an increased threat of nuclear war between them, and NATO, Russia, and China were on high alert.

"It's beginning," Kris said.

Kris retreated to her diary, a safe refuge from the chaos.

Tuesday, July 24, 2035. Ant's not waking up. It makes me sick. Not knowing what will happen to her is worse than anything. Maybe she will never get better.

We're ready to talk to the orb in Times Square. Before now, language had been simple to me. Just communication. Nothing more. Nate has always said that mathematics is the universal language. But what does that mean? If math is universal, then is it the only possible method of communication with other sentient species? What if they don't have mouths and can't talk? What if they don't have ears to listen or eyes to see the way humans do? Sign language and body language would be lost on them. The M-Team and all the other scientists working on this alien puzzle are in the dark about what they're like.

Do the aliens have souls, even?

Kris wandered to the workroom and found Benedita sitting silent with her eyes closed and her hands folded before her.

"Sorry to interrupt. I can leave if you'd like," Kris said.

Benedita opened her eyes as if emerging from a deep trance. "It's fine. I wouldn't mind the company."

Kris sat next to her. "Were you praying?"

"Yeah." Her face lit up, and she was happy to share her faith. "I don't mind admitting it. We need all the help we can get."

"I agree with that."

"Do you believe in God?" Benedita asked, as if she were asking Kris her favorite color or ice cream flavor.

Kris was speechless. It was a sincere question, one that made an odd kind of sense just then, when the world was teetering on the edge of the abyss. In trying times, people tended to find comfort in religion or faith.

"To be honest," Kris said, "I don't know. But I would say no, I don't believe in a higher power. My logical brain can't make sense of religion."

"I see. I was raised Catholic, though I'm not a good one. I don't often pray or go to mass."

"If there is a God, then I wish He would help us now."

Benedita looked surprised. "How do you know God is male? I don't think God has a gender. It's our language with its anthropomorphic tendencies that implies that."

"Sometimes I wonder if we talk ourselves into thinking things are real just because we can describe them. I doubt the aliens think of language that way," Kris said. She had the sinking feeling they'd soon find out.

"Their language is mathematics," Benedita said. "I'm sure they find our spoken languages baffling, the same way they'd find our culture strange. For all its armies, the military can't do much without *us*, without the people who think about things deeply."

Kris liked Benedita. She spoke her mind. That took guts.

"It must be pissing the generals off," Kris responded.

"Yes. They've met their match, their own higher power that they cannot attack."

"Do you think we have a chance? A chance of making this work?"

"I hope so," Benedita said. "Are you worried that we don't?"

"Perhaps. I suppose now is as good a time as any to have faith."

"Would you like to join me in a prayer?"

"I don't know how. I've never prayed before."

"Close your eyes and ask for something. Try to be humble when you petition God for mercy."

Kris closed her eyes with Benedita, feeling odd. The orb's message flashed in her mind. *I direct this prayer to the orb aliens. If you can hear me in the nexus, or wherever you live, please bring Sarah back and talk to us.*

She wasn't sure who she was talking to. God. The aliens. Or herself. Anger boiled up inside her. Her face flushed.

Also...I hate you for all of this. My sister is in a coma because of you, and my mom is missing. Couldn't you have said hi without causing all this madness?

Kris waited for a response, but there was none. She hadn't expected them to answer.

◎ ◦ ◎

Yolanda received orders to leave that morning. Her father insisted that in light of the ever-expanding global crisis, the family should be together. No one knew what would happen when the M-Team attempted to communicate with the orb, and General Choi wasn't taking any chances with his daughter. The major public officials, heads of state, or royal houses were being kept far away. There was a press conference that morning during which Nate explained to the public what they'd attempt to do in Times Square.

Now they had little choice but to do it.

If India and Pakistan were about to engage in a full-blown nuclear conflict, then there was a high risk of that destabilization spreading to other nations. The president of the United States gave an address from the Oval Office after the press conference, and she was whisked away to a secure location soon afterward.

With all the military personnel going with the M-Team, the base would go into shutdown mode with a skeletal staff. Already, the place was barren. The echoes of her footsteps down the long white halls startled her. The M-Team, while exhausted, readied themselves to meet the orb. None of them had been close to one except for Kris. Despite their questions, she was reluctant to talk about her experience. Reluctant to talk, period, with Antoinette's recent tragedy fresh in her mind.

Yolanda was at the door.

"Oh, wow. Wasn't General Choi insisting that you leave?"

"I told him to jump in a lake, plus a few more words I don't want to repeat. He treats me like a child, but I'm not."

Kris hugged her tight. For a brief moment, she was safe. She was home.

"Stop it, Einstein. You're gonna make me cry again. I wouldn't miss tonight for anything. After all, if you can't talk to the little green men, then I'm guessing there's nowhere safe to hide. I'd rather be there with you to the end."

Kris had a strange sense of connection with Yolanda. She was out of place here in this group of mathematicians, much like how Kris used to feel like an outsider among girls her age.

She shuddered. The world was changing. She was changing. Now Kris was on the inside looking out. She'd never been included before. Maybe this was what it was to be an adult.

Kris and Yolanda walked to their bedrooms one last time. This place—this awful, cold place—had been their home for the last few days. Kris was reluctant to leave its protective enclosure. Antoinette would remain at the base and receive round-the-clock care. Kris stopped by to see her before they left.

"We're off, Ant. I promise I'll be back soon."

Antoinette lay in silence, as if she were deeply asleep. Her breathing was rhythmic and calming.

"I'll get Mom back too. And something else..." She reached over and touched her sister's hand. It was soft and warm. "It was always me who was jealous of you. You were always the stronger one."

Nate had asked Kris to visit him before they all headed out, and when she reached his office, he was putting papers into a briefcase.

"We ready?" she asked.

"Yes, we're ready. As ready as we'll ever be."

"What happens if we fail?"

"No idea. I haven't gotten that far, to be honest."

"If we have to leave, what happens? Do we keep working from here?

"I could lie and say yes, but you need to understand—we may get only one shot at this."

"It has to work," Kris insisted. Nate responded with silence.

Kris sighed and pulled her fingers through her hair. The uncertainty of it all ate away at her. The team was to gather at what they called the "great shell" around the orb in Times Square. Twenty feet high, it was made of giant screens divided into four equal-sized parts. There were gaps between the screens where they could see the orb.

They'd recorded part of the message to play to the aliens. The rest had to be sent live, one person per screen, in case the response changed or needed to adapt. Using the infinite-dimensional computer model Kris and Lara had created, they'd encoded the last proof that morning. Kris knew their response was correct, but she couldn't see beyond that.

The whole M-Team would be there in person at the direct request of Four. Nate had opposed the idea, citing safety concerns. What if the orbs glowed red again and made all of their experts vanish? But the order was clear. There was a strong likelihood that the aliens would respond in real time, and no one could trust a computer to carry on a conversation with them properly.

Nate turned serious. "We'll be depending on you, Kris. You're the brightest of us. If things go south, you'll need to intervene."

"You expect me to *improvise* with an infinite alien intelligence?"

"They have infinite storage, and they know a heck of a lot of mathematics. More than we could uncover in ten thousand years. Nevertheless, I believe with absolute certainty that they're like us—just explorers in search of other sentient species."

Kris hoped he was right. If they'd wanted to come to Earth simply to blow up humanity, they could have done that ages ago in a much simpler way. They were clearly hoping to talk. Kris just wasn't sure what she'd say to them.

"What about the others? Will they be able to talk to the aliens too?"

"Yes, of course. And I'll be there monitoring, and we'll have the support of the secondary and tertiary groups. But there may come a moment when our backs are against the wall and we don't have time to discuss or analyze anything, just *act*."

The scope of it was hard to conceive. Kris imagined the future if they didn't succeed. She put her hand to her chin. Many major cities had orbs sitting in them. If the aliens were trying to get their attention, it was working.

◎ ∘ ◎

Kris watched the clock on her phone. She grabbed her backpack and stuffed her diary inside. There was no looking back now.

The preparations at Times Square were concluding, according to Nate. The team would roll out at four in the afternoon, leaving the engineers at the orb enough time to calibrate the instruments before their arrival. Kris had insisted on riding with Yolanda. Nate had wanted them in separate trucks for security reasons, but Kris wouldn't hear of it. They'd made it this far together. Yolanda had won out against her general father and stayed at the base, so she too was part of the strange caravan that descended on the empty city.

"Do you think they have green skin and three eyes?" Yolanda asked.

"No. I'm not sure they have skin or eyes at all," Kris said.

"Ten fingers?"

"Maybe twenty-eight fingers. Or none."

Yolanda didn't respond, just looked pensively out the window. Antoinette's coma was an ever-present pulse below the surface, shared between them.

"I wish my sister were here," Kris said.

Yolanda's eyes were glassy.

"At least she's alive because of you."

"I'm no hero. I did what anyone would have done." Yolanda reached for Kris's hand and squeezed it.

Private Dax drove them to New York City, the two of them in the back of the black electric SUV. He tapped an app on the console and took his hands off the wheel as the vehicle sped along using its driverless tech. Kris expected that this trip would be like the last time she'd visited New York, but with more comfort than the small, cramped back of a truck. It was a brilliant sunny day, and she could feel the heat outside even through the tinted windows. The coolness of the air conditioning was artificial, metallic against her skin. She placed her hand on the sun-warmed window.

The road ahead was desolate, with no traffic other than the caravan of SUVs and trucks. A helicopter flew above them, almost out of sight.

"We'll be there soon enough," Private Dax said, staring at Kris in the rearview mirror.

No looking back. Kris had made up her mind that she wasn't going to run away this time. She was going to face the future, no matter what it brought.

CHAPTER 12

YOU ARE READY

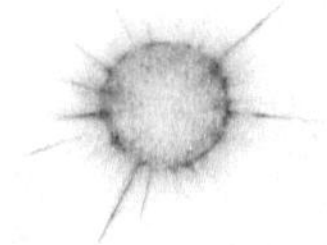

"WE'RE IN THE Big Apple," Yolanda said.

Kris scratched her head and peered out the window. She'd been rereading calculations in her diary and had lost track of time.

They crossed a large bridge, with the city skyline in clear view ahead. Convoys of vehicles slid by, windows blacked out, their sensor rigs blinking like fireflies. Kris's last memory of New York was leaving it with Antoinette. Times Square and the orb. Five days had passed since she'd visited the orb, but to her it felt like a thousand glacial years.

Within half an hour, the cavalcade had descended on the scientific base in Times Square. There must have been several hundred soldiers, engineers, and scientists all preparing for what was to come. It would be the M-Team's turn soon.

Kris's insides turned to Jell-O. She was scared of failing, scared of being too stupid, scared of letting Sarah and Antoinette down.

What if we fail? What if I fail? she thought.

Nate greeted Kris as she and Yolanda exited the SUV, bringing with him a small entourage—two men and a woman she didn't recognize.

"Kris, I want you to meet the leaders of the secondary and tertiary teams, Dr. Makassarian and Dr. Cheung. And this is Dr. Major, who's been analyzing the orb since it appeared in New York."

Kris shook their hands.

"It's such an honor to meet you, Dr. Argentia. Dr. Wallace said you're the brightest mathematician he's ever met, and I'd have to agree," Cheung said, smiling broadly.

Kris said a quiet "Thank you."

Dr. Major said nothing, but he stared at her in a way that made her shiver as if she'd been hit with an invisible wave of frost. There was a tiny pin on his shirt of three orange-and-yellow-striped flowers, their curved green stems facing downward.

"There will be a meeting at seven p.m. of the M-Team and the support staff in the workroom," Nate said. "Diya will come around to collect you. You'll have to excuse me now; I have to attend to other matters."

Kris noticed Toor in the distance giving orders to a group of half a dozen of her agents. Their eyes met for a second, and Toor acknowledged her with the slightest tilt of her head.

Kris marveled at her surroundings. Dozens of scientists walked around in white lab coats, taking readings and communicating on their tablets. Engineers worked on the great shell, which the M-Team would use to try and communicate with the aliens. Dozens of soldiers buzzed around the area, helicopters circled in the sky, and tanks sat at each main intersection. The occasional jet passed overhead.

At the center of it was the orb, now partially hidden by the curved shell. Kris made her way toward it, fumbling through the crowd swarming around it. From a distance, the shell looked whole, but as Kris drew closer, the structure resolved into four massive panels, reaching twenty feet up. Each panel was curved like a segment of a ring and arranged symmetrically around the orb. Narrow gaps, several feet wide and evenly spaced, allowed for partial views of the alien artifact.

It had a dark, hard-looking exterior, a few inches thick. The shell's material was unusual. Kris had never seen anything like it—jet-black, but with fine patterns of gray lines riddling its surface. Beyond the shell, at measured distances from each gap, sat four small recessed stations arranged like points on a compass.

She was about twenty-five feet from the shell when a nearby soldier told her that she couldn't get any closer. Kris strained her neck to catch a glimpse of the orb. She could see a small segment of it through a vertical opening in the shell.

"There are screens on the inside. The most sophisticated screens ever engineered, at least on this planet," said Dr. Major, coming up to stand beside her. He grabbed her arm and leaned over to speak quietly into her ear.

"Don't trust Four. They're not what they appear to be," he said, glancing sideways.

Kris pushed him away and stared at him in disbelief. He walked past her, pretending to have said nothing. A deep chill hit Kris, as if she'd walked into a freezer. How much *did* she know about Toor's team? What was their true purpose?

Nate had told Kris that the M-Team's messages would be projected onto those screens for the orb to view. And even now, engineers in blue overalls worked away at the shell, tuning it for its purpose. Kris wondered if the orb could see them. Would it understand their primitive attempt to communicate? The questions made her uneasy.

The M-Team would sit around the outside of the shell at equidistant stations that would allow them to communicate their complex codes to one another and to the orb via Nate. He'd be the grand maestro, feeding the team's response to the orb. Images, based on their limited understanding of the alien cipher, would populate the inside of the shell. Kris visualized them as virtuosos in a mathematical symphony. It made her laugh, as she'd never played an instrument before, even though Sarah had hounded her for years to try. Then there was the ethereal music that permeated her mind when she did math, coming from nowhere and everywhere. Maybe she would hear that again.

Kris fidgeted with her notes in a large tent made of light beige canvas near the shell. It was bright with the lights on, and she surrounded herself with screens displaying various parts of the message. She studied and restudied each line of the proof of the Riemann hypothesis like she were cramming for an exam.

"Hey, Einstein," Yolanda said, peering into the folds of the tent door. She looked different today; she wore no makeup and had her hair pulled back. She'd traded her dresses and jewelry for black shorts and a plain gray T-shirt.

"My little buddy would cheer you up." Yolanda handed Cindi to her, and the dog's eyebrows twitched from side to side as she wagged her tail. Kris scratched behind her ears.

"I'm glad you came," Kris said.

"Me too. There's no way I would leave you alone to do this," Yolanda responded. She stood close to her, and the air hummed.

Kris stared at her like she was seeing Yolanda for the first time. She'd shed her skin, all her layers peeled back. And there she was, just a girl with eyes beaming like binary stars.

"What happens next?" Kris asked.

"You're going to work. I'm going to call my brother. Cindi will keep you company," Yolanda said.

"*Miigwech*. That means thank you in Ojibwe," Kris said. Yolanda gave Kris a peck on the cheek before she left.

Kris returned to studying her proof, this time with renewed intensity. Cindi panted on her lap, a warm ball of fur. The proof was so complex, but she charged on.

Agent Diya entered the tent to collect her. Yolanda waited for her outside, talking in hushed tones to her brother on her phone. Cindi ran to Yolanda, and she cradled the dog in her free arm as she spoke. Kris walked with her arm locked around Yolanda to the meeting called by Nate and the M-Team. Some of the agents protested, but Yolanda refused to leave Kris's side. Kris argued that she was as much a part of the team as anyone else. She'd possibly saved Kris's life. Nate intervened to let her stay.

This gathering would be the final one before their attempt at communication. Nate would lead the discussion. Would he be able to navigate this important role? He could be so selfish. Kris hoped he could put the needs of the group ahead of his own ambition.

"We're all here now, so let's begin," Nate said into a mic. The packed tent contained the M-Team, the secondary and tertiary teams, scientists like Dr. Major, and a large, assorted collection of military commanders. His deep voice filled up the space well, she thought. Kris felt small, seated on Nate's left side, Toor on his right.

"We're here for one reason and one reason only: to communicate with the aliens and get our people back. Assembled here are our best mathematical, scientific, and engineering minds, each of whom has been working toward this goal. We've made incredible progress toward deciphering the alien message, and our main discovery was that of an infinite-dimensional code inherent in the message. In response, we've developed a prototype of an infinite-dimensional computer based on the team's mathematical ideas, which has allowed us to access some—*some*—of the contents of the code.

"For the mathematical laypeople, the aliens have stored an infinite amount of knowledge, exclusively mathematical from what we can tell, within the hidden dimensions of the message they've sent us. We conjecture that this is a kind of galactic greeting from the extraterrestrial intelligence behind the orbs. It's tailored to gauge the level of mathematical maturity of the species it interacts with."

Nate's voice became more emphatic as murmurs sifted through the crowd. "Within the section of the message we can understand, we've isolated parts that are unlike the others."

The message flashed on a large screen behind him, morphing into the code the M-Team had discovered. Within their code, there were chunks of red symbols. Each of these expanded one by one to reveal various formulas on the screen.

"What you're viewing are questions. Conjectures. Theorems.

These are prompts for us to respond to with solutions or proofs. Each part is more complex than the last, escalating in difficulty as we move through the code. The final question is focused on the Riemann hypothesis, which many consider to be the deepest conjecture in all of mathematics. This conjecture was unsolved until recently, when it was proven by Dr. Kris Argentia."

All eyes moved to Kris like lasers converging on a focal point. She could own this proof now. She had to.

Nate continued, explaining how the first goal would be to broadcast a kind of primer through the great shell. This should get the aliens' attention. It would show them that humans grasped the introductory part of the message. The M-Team would enter the code for each subsequent part in real time. The secondary and tertiary teams would relay this information, encoding each message into the alien language. The great shell surrounding the orb would then display the messages. The screen behind Nate showed a short time-lapse movie of the shell and its construction. It ended with a live image of workers tinkering with it even as they spoke.

"Communication will begin at midnight, after final calibrations on the shell are complete," Nate said. "Godspeed to those involved in this work. This will likely be our one chance to communicate with the aliens. We can only trust that it'll be enough and that they'll bring our people back to us."

After the meeting ended and people poured out of the tent, Kris sat with Yolanda. Cindi barked and licked her hand. Kris welcomed Yolanda's company, even if the mood was dark. Silence hung between them for a while, and then Kris said, "Let's hope Nate is right and our assumptions are correct. The aliens came demanding answers. I hope we have the right ones."

"I've seen a lot," Yolanda said, "but what's happening right now is scary. Last December, turning eighteen was scary. Nothing I ever imagined compares to alien orbs."

Kris put her hand on Yolanda's shoulder.

"Antoinette believes in you too," Yolanda said.

Kris repressed the flood of emotions that always came upon hearing her sister's name. She hoped the M-Team was right, for all their sakes. Her life had flipped upside down since the orbs had arrived a week ago. She hoped it was time to set things right.

"Listen, I need to ask you a favor," Kris said.

She whispered in her ear, and Yolanda pulled back, eyes wide with disbelief.

"You can tell her that yourself," Yolanda said.

A pang hit Kris's heart. She said nothing.

Yolanda's face softened, and her eyes locked onto Kris's with silent understanding.

After Yolanda left, Kris lay on a cot to rest. She closed her eyes, surrendering to the fatigue that made her body ache.

Riddled with dizzying currents of light, the orb beamed out patterns in every direction, making her squint as she sat below it in the grassy meadow. There was a rushing sound, cold and fierce, like water running nearby.

"Maker is ready. She will come with the pattern we seek."

Kris lay on the cool, wet grass. Above her, the orb floated and shimmered. All around it were stars. Every star grew brighter, turning into an orb, pulsing across the night sky in a delicate web of patterns. Like the network of orbs in the nexus. Deep inside, in her bones, she was ready.

"Kris."

The voice startled her. It wasn't the orb. She bolted upright and ran through the dark grassy meadow barefoot, the long blades of grass tickling her toes.

Ari stood by the river, dressed in a crisp white button-down shirt and white pants, also barefoot. Kris's hands tingled from the cool breeze coming from the direction of the river.

She woke with a gasp and had no clue where she was. Reality flowed back in slowly, like a hose filling a kiddie pool. She was alone in a military tent in Times Square, hours away from their attempt to talk to the orbs and bring Sarah back. She grabbed her phone from a side table, and it lit up the beige tarp around her—eight twelve p.m. Kris threw on her shoes and pulled her hair back in a ponytail. She had to speak with Toor.

Kris darted through the rows of tents, asking an officer to find Toor's. A light flickered inside one of them, and she heard Toor's familiar commanding voice.

"Did you bring *him* here?" Kris said breathlessly, barging in on a meeting Toor was having with her agents.

Toor paused. She gave a slight nod, and the agents scattered like bees. She understood that Kris was talking about Ari.

"I had to keep him safe, and it's safer here now than anywhere else. He's under constant guard, however, so don't be worried. How did you know he was here?"

"That doesn't matter. Where is he?"

Toor's shoulders lifted. "I don't think it's a good idea for you to see him right now."

Kris stood her ground and glared at Toor, who stood tall, all CIA and secret agent–like. Toor matched her gaze. There was a long silence.

"You know I'm not budging until I see Ari."

"All right. But I'm coming with you," she said.

Kris walked behind Toor and ducked her head as she entered the tent. There was a lamp filling it with a soft yellow glow, and humidity hung in the air.

Ari sat up on the bed, causing Agent Diya, who was standing guard, to take one short step forward. Toor lifted her right index finger, and he stepped back. Diya stood tall and immovable, like Toor and her agents tended to do.

"Holy crap. I didn't think they would let me see you. I'm so, *so* sorry about Antoinette. I never meant—"

Kris shook her head, silencing him. She wanted to lunge and hit him, strangle him. It took every ounce of control to do nothing.

"You don't even get to say her name." Her lips pursed, and she dug her fingernails into her palms. His eyes were soft, but there was fear there. He shot a glance at Toor.

"I need to know something, and only you can tell me for sure." Kris's mind raced as she catapulted back to that horrible scene. She could feel his grip on her arm, see Antoinette falling, see her platinum hair damp with blood. She cringed at the mental image.

Toor grew rigid. Kris leaned forward.

"Tell me about your dreams, Ari." Kris sat in the lone chair, some six feet away from him. She exhaled and let her shoulders drop. He closed his eyes as if in a trance.

"There were lots. They came in bunches, especially after I saw the patterns on the orb in Toronto. One thing kept coming back, though. Over and over, like it was on a loop." His voice grew distant. "I was in a giant field filled with grass. There was an orb there, floating."

Kris swallowed, her throat tight. She could smell the grass. See that web of patterns. Hear the rushing sound of water.

He was describing her dream! A sudden coldness gripped her.

"The orb was talking nonsense about the Maker. I tried to follow it but couldn't. I figured it was talking about me, but I was wrong." He rubbed his hand against his face and let out a sigh.

"There was another person there, hidden in the field. I never saw them, but I heard them. You've gotta believe me."

Kris sat back. She looked up at Toor, whose face was grim, like she'd seen a ghost.

"I'm sorry. Believe me, I'm sorry," Ari begged.

Kris began to head outside, then stopped. She turned to Ari, whose face was wet with tears. What he'd done was monstrous. He should have stopped and left before things got so bad. He should have backed away when Antoinette threatened him. There were a million ways the situation could have been different. But Kris didn't think he'd intentionally tried to put Ant in a coma. That didn't lessen her anger, but it put it into perspective.

Kris held his gaze. "I believe you. But if my sister dies or wakes up broken because of you, I'll never forgive you. Not ever."

His face went cold. Her cheeks flushed red-hot, and she walked out.

What did Toor know? Kris paced outside the tent, kicking at a page from a newspaper lying on the ground, until she emerged. The flap of the tent closed behind Toor, and she stood across from Kris with folded arms.

"Why is Ari having dreams like me?" Kris asked.

Toor was silent as a statue for a long minute. Her eyes were darker than normal and icicle-cold.

"That took guts," she finally said. "We're alike, you know. You've got all the qualities of a leader."

Kris remained silent.

Toor continued, "When Four first instructed us to include you in the M-Team, I had my doubts. I studied your bio with amazement—how you learned calculus at the age of ten, then began your doctorate at thirteen. You are one of our brightest mathematical minds on the planet, but I was still skeptical that a teenager could help us to communicate with an alien race. I was wrong about you."

"You're good at not answering questions," Kris said.

Toor laughed. "And you're adept at hacking my communications."

Kris's mouth opened, but she couldn't think of a thing to say.

"Did you think we didn't know? My team alerted me the moment you entered my folders. It's our business to know about such intrusions," Toor said with an arrogant light in her eyes.

"So you just showed me what you wanted me to see?" Kris asked.

Toor was a mystery to Kris, even after all this time. Who was she, and what did she want?

"What is at coordinates 13.9°S 59.2°W?"

"Valles Marineris," Toor said.

"Of course; not on Earth, but on Mars," Kris muttered. Where humanity first encountered the orbs.

"We're going to try to talk to the aliens," Kris said. "We might only get one shot at this. If we mess it up, that's it. I'll never see Mom again."

Her voice tightened. "So how am I supposed to do this if you're not telling me everything?"

Toor's eyes closed to a sliver. "I understand that. And I have faith in you and the M-Team. But you know what you need to know."

A helicopter thudded overhead, the sound echoing off the darkened buildings. Kris shifted her weight and slid her hands into the pockets of her jeans, her fingers closing around her pen. She rolled it back and forth, resisting the urge to snap it.

"Ari's hurting in there," she said. "He's been hurting for a long time, and you didn't notice. Help him."

Toor's left eye twitched, and her gaze softened. Kris saw the mother in her before the mask snapped back into place.

"Some minds line up with the orbs and their dream-mediated communication better than others," Toor said. "Your advanced mathematical mind did. His didn't. That's my best guess."

Toor rubbed her thumb against the side of her finger, a small, restless motion. Kris turned to walk away. One thing was certain now.

I can't fail, Kris thought.

She headed for the great shell, where the M-Team was already gathering.

Kris gathered with the other M-Team members, arranged around the orb. It was close to midnight. They were in an unorthodox orchestra pit. What a bizarre symphony they would play. While they weren't too close to the orb itself, they were close enough to feel the vibration Kris had described when she'd stood next to it on her earlier trip to Times Square.

It was a song. Like the music she'd always heard in her mind.

"I know you can feel it too. We all can," Benedita said in a serious tone.

Kris and the M-Team members stood at a console with a large screen projected in front of them. She could only make out Benedita on her right, with Luke and Lara hidden by the shell. The light of the screen illuminated her face, making her look like a ghost. They all wore wireless headsets that would let them talk to each other without leaving their stations. Behind them was the backdrop of a blackened Times Square and a canopy of stars. The area was filled with an eerie quietness and emptiness so uncharacteristic of the place.

"I felt the vibrations way stronger before, when I was alone with the orb," Kris said to Benedita. "It's like something is singing to us."

"You know about the music of the spheres, the *musica universalis*? It goes back to Pythagoras, who said he could hear it and that it helped him compute musical ratios to the motions of celestial objects."

"I've heard it when I'm proving theorems," Kris said. She

stopped, choosing her words. "Usually the tough ones. The sound doesn't have a place. It's just…everywhere."

She had never told that to anyone before. She was certain now that the music was *real*. Maybe the orb aliens had been singing to humans throughout history, ever since they'd made their first cave drawings.

Benedita glanced sideways at Kris. The orb was like a black hole, tugging at them with infinite gravity. Her panicky sensation came back. She resisted the urge to run and chose a large number to factor into primes to get her mind off the orb.

Why? Why be afraid? Kris wondered.

The orb spoke in math. That should have comforted her. Instead, it terrified her. She pushed her anxiety aside. They had a job to do.

Kris and the other members of the M-Team sat waiting around the great shell. Nate was outside the central circle at his console, which had a swirling dance of charts, plots, and formulae projected on a large screen behind him for all to see. He was like the conductor, weaving complete forms and patterns from the separate sections of the orchestra. Toor stood, watching, by his side, with Agent Diya beside her, looking grave.

Behind Kris were the secondary and tertiary teams. The military encircled all of them; Yolanda sat with the soldiers. General Choi had come to the square to be with her. He was tall, with short pepper-gray hair and sharp eyes. He'd convinced her to watch the proceedings from the outermost ring, but Kris knew she would have preferred to be up close with the M-Team.

"On my mark, activation," said Nate over the loudspeaker. "Three, two, one…activate."

"Here we go," Kris said over her mic. She bit her fingernails. The process of communicating with the aliens was about to begin.

On cue, the lights around the command post dimmed to a mild glow. The great shell lit up with patterns and images that mimicked the message the orb had broadcast, though now it sat silent and black as ever.

"Tertiary teams, activate," Nate ordered.

Those in the outer rings began sending their message out. They relayed the preliminary message—a kind of introduction using the alien symbology. Kris hoped they had it right.

The message flashed on both sides of the shell, which was translucent, but the orb stayed dark. Austere. Ambivalent to the carnival of lights.

"Secondary teams, activate."

Now for the big assumption. Kris gripped the sides of her screen. Their ideas about the infinite-dimensional computer had to be correct. They would find out any minute, one way or another.

The message on the shell splintered in a million directions, displaying vast, complex patterns that folded in on themselves. The screen behind Nate mimicked these patterns, but on its flat surface. After numerous iterations, an order arose, which was the effect of the new high-dimensional algorithms. Kris could see her work and that of the team as the patterns broke into the ten hidden parts of the message in an unmistakable crimson red.

Every passing second felt like a year. She looked up and scanned the M-Team, barely visible to her. Lara coughed. The orb made a brief pulse. There was a crackle over Kris's earpiece, and it startled her. She wondered if she'd made a mistake.

"We're waiting. Say something," Kris whispered.

She grabbed her diary from her backpack and flipped to a page with a bookmark. The proof of the Riemann hypothesis was there in summarized form. She traced her index finger over the calculations, rechecking each one. She knew them by heart, but she had to be sure. If she'd entered them correctly in the display, then it should work. But there was no manual, no instructions to guide them. They were attempting to communicate with an alien species.

Another pulse.

Kris bit her lip. The orb was pitch-black again.

"It's working! We're getting through to them. Do you see it?" she said into her mic.

"Yes, of course I do. We're on track for the most important step," Nate said. His voice conveyed its typical arrogance, but Kris could hear the excitement there too.

After a silence that lasted an eternity, Nate ordered, "Primary teams, activate."

Kris's breath came faster. Time quickened.

One by one, the team began sending their messages. The orb remained blank, as black as the ominous night sky above. Kris's nerves were raw as the progression of messages crept toward her own: the Riemann hypothesis and its proof. The full proof would have taken hours to translate, but the team had distilled the key ideas and turned them into digestible pieces. Kris could now write out the main steps in a few minutes.

It was her turn. She hesitated as if her finger were on the trigger of a gun. She knew this was the best mathematical idea they had in their arsenal—the best idea the *human race* had. Her proof would clinch the communication with orbs. It all fell on her.

"Hurry up, Kris. We need your code now," Nate said.

With care and attention, she keyed in the condensed proof of the Riemann hypothesis. Her entering it live was the essential key. It took longer than she'd expected: a full ten minutes to encode the short sketch of the proof.

Collectively, they waited. Kris put her head in her hands as she watched for a response. Seconds turned into minutes. Benedita closed her eyes as if in meditation. It was so quiet that even the slightest sound was amplified through their headsets.

The orb remained silent. Kris wondered if she'd made an error, and she tapped a pen on the screen. Her nerves were raw. Nate's face was stoic, his gaze fixated on readings on his screen.

After twenty minutes, Kris could make out subtle white spots appearing on the orb. Only a few at first. But they began to cluster, coalescing into new patterns.

Seconds later, the orb was on fire, like a million fireflies dancing in the summer sky, all of which were different from anything they'd seen before.

"We need to respond. Now!" Nate screamed to the M-Team.

"How? It's too fast. I can't follow any of it," Kris said.

"We need translation."

Following instructions from the secondary team, the translation software within the shell activated, revealing a similar blizzard of symbols. Text rose on Kris's screen. Her mind reeled at the volume of information. Mathematical text, reams of it, scrolled past. She struggled to find a part she recognized. Kris discovered a block of familiar-looking text, and her heart leapt. She zoomed in on it with her fingers.

"I get this part—block fifty A. I can respond," Kris said.

"Do it," Nate said.

Kris dove into the block, pulling it apart until it was in smaller chunks.

"I'm on one forty-two B," said Luke.

"Twenty-seven C," said Benedita.

The M-Team began to respond as best they could to the messages emanating from the orb. Bit by bit, they were tackling the alien's challenge. Benedita let out a long sigh beside her.

For half an hour, messages poured out of the orb, and the shell relayed the team's responses in an orderly fashion. Kris, immersed in the symphony, watched in wonder. It was a mathematical duet going back and forth between the orb and the team. The mathematics in the messages was becoming much more complicated, and it arrived after shorter and shorter intervals. The orb was probing them, testing their abilities and resolve. So far, the M-Team had responded to more than fifty different queries.

They were communicating with an alien race.

Kris could feel sweat forming on her neck as she tried to keep up with the questions emerging from the orb. This was no longer a one-way street. It was a *conversation*. The first time something like this had ever happened.

Without warning, the orb stopped flashing. All messages ceased.

The team focused on their screens. Like Kris, they weren't sure if the orb had merely paused or if the messages had finished.

"I'm not sure I could have kept that up much longer," Kris said to herself as she gazed up at the silent orb. *Please be done*, she thought.

"We've done it," Nate concluded, speaking over the headsets. "We've had our first successful communication with an alien species."

A cheer came from the teams and the soldiers. The team and soldiers gave each other high fives and handshakes. Kris let her head fall. Her fingers were burning, and she was shaking from the mental exertion. Nate began congratulating the team, moving to each person in turn. Kris slouched, wanting nothing more than to curl into a ball and sleep.

Then she heard it through her headphones. A faint noise, like a whisper across a dark hallway or a child's footsteps on dew-covered grass.

"Do you hear that?" Kris asked. Benedita lifted her head, listening. At first, Kris took it for feedback from the speakers or part of the computer translation. But it became louder with each passing moment—the voices, the music. Like in her dreams. Like when she'd made physical contact with the orb in Times Square. She felt a dull shock as she recalled the multitude of voices in her dreams.

Kris heard Cindi barking. Someone screamed—Yolanda. The orb let off a reddish glow. Her biggest fear was coming true. Kris's shock gave way to panic.

Nate shook his head. "No, no, no! We did everything right." He gripped the control screen.

A siren went off, and soldiers started moving. Evacuation instructions boomed through the headsets and over the loudspeakers. Nate frantically keyed codes into his console. The members of the M-Team had already begun running from their consoles, as did the members of the secondary and tertiary groups. An empty band of space, free of people, formed around the orb, like a wave expanding outward from a ripple in a pond.

They ran. All of them ran from what they didn't understand. Except one.

Kris walked toward the orb instead, passing through a gap in the shell. She had to speak to it without a filter, without a barrier.

Yolanda cried out, and Kris looked behind her in a daze. Yolanda ran toward her, gesturing wildly for her to get back. Agent Diya grabbed her, holding Yolanda in place as she struggled. Kris wanted to retreat, to find safety with the others, but she had no control of her body as she walked toward the orb.

"Wait!" Nate screamed in her ear.

Kris took off the headset and let it fall from her fingers, and it fell to the ground in slow motion like snowflakes. *I can't go back now.*

Kris stopped before the orb, standing inches away from its smooth surface. Her mind was full of the orb's energy, its ideas. Its song. She reached out to touch it—smooth like glass. It gave off no warmth despite the angry red hue tarnishing its surface.

"Hello? Can you hear me?" Kris asked.

Nothing changed.

"The Maker's here. The Maker is back with the pattern you seek. I'm not running away anymore." Kris merely mouthed the words as she called out to the aliens in her mind. All her choices had brought her to this point. She wasn't backing down now.

Her hand glowed translucent where it touched the surface of the orb, and there was a surge, like an electric charge with no pain. She closed her eyes and focused all her attention.

"We're here. We're alive. Please don't harm us. Please return our people to us. It isn't their fault that they don't understand you. But I do. We do. Please."

Kris was inside a hurricane. With her eyes closed, she could see them—the patterns, broken, coalescing. They hurt like hell. She didn't know she could hurt so much. Mathematical concepts the likes of which she'd never seen flooded into her mind. She tried to block the flood of concepts, but they were like knives inside her brain. Her legs were like Jell-O as she lowered herself to a crouch, her hand glued to the orb. She tried to resist, but she was slipping deeper inside the orb's influence. To her, there was nothing left in the world except the sound.

"You are ready," the voices in her mind wailed.

Vaguely, Kris could hear Yolanda screaming. She screamed too, inside. She wanted to run away, but her body would not obey. She blinked, and the people, the sounds, the movements around her were reduced to a garble of complex patterns, not unlike those on the orb's surface. The orb sparkled as if its surface were covered in diamonds and rubies and emeralds.

"I'm like you. Please talk to me," Kris said.

"Kris!" Yolanda's faint voice was a million miles away, a ripple on the surface of the sea of patterns.

Nothing mattered anymore except the voices in her mind.

Kris opened her eyes. Her mom stood beside her. Kris relaxed and stopped resisting the pull of the orb.

There was a white flash.

CHAPTER 13
HOME

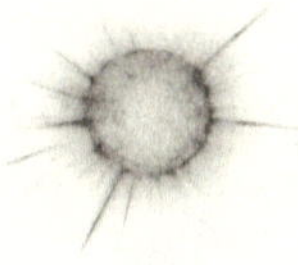

K RIS FELL FORWARD into a familiar place that was no place. She jolted as Times Square disappeared in an instant. She was floating in space. A rush of mathematical awareness spiraled around her, with millions of beaming white orbs hanging like ornaments in an infinite blackness. They each had a name that no human could say. This was the place she had seen on her first visit to the orb, the strange place where the orb aliens lived.

The nexus.

She'd seen her mom before she left the square. Her mom was alive! Kris hugged herself with happiness. The rest of the vanished people were back too. She'd felt them return.

Now she was back in their world.

Music roared in her chest as the white braid blazed in the distance. Every bit of mathematical knowledge was there, beckoning her forward with its music. She wanted to join it as she had before.

"You are ready," the voices echoed from nowhere and from everywhere. "Choose."

Yes, of course, she thought. Kris closed her eyes. There was no uncertainty left. The road behind her led straight to this.

Memories poured in like sunlight breaking through storm

clouds. They came in fragments, only half formed but fresh and sparkling. Antoinette sang "Nothing but the Stars," strumming her guitar. Sarah mouthed, "Go get 'em," at the beginning of her doctoral defense. Harold the fat cat purred on her lap outside their tiny bungalow. Sand scratched her toes as she walked barefoot on Woodbine Beach in the July sun. The intense smell of black coffee from The Uncommon lingered in her nostrils. Her diary, cluttered with equations, lay open on a messy desk, ETC staring back from his picture on the wall.

Kris knew now what she had to do.

"Please, help my sister," she said.

The orbs pulsed in brilliant white light around her.

Another white flash.

Kris froze and stared. She materialized in a hospital room where her mom slept by Antoinette's side. Slivers of yellow light through the shuttered window revealed that it was daytime, though the lights were dim.

"Mom?" Kris said, placing her hand on Sarah's shoulder.

Sarah jolted awake and looked up at her, her gaze bleary. Her face contorted as comprehension dawned, and she grabbed Kris, her arms like a vise as she pulled Kris into a warm hug. They wept as they held each other.

"I knew I could bring you back. I knew I would find you," Kris's voice cracked.

"Where did you go? I saw you in Times Square, and then you vanished. For days."

Kris paused. "Time must've flowed differently for me."

"We're in a place in D.C. run by Agent Toor," Sarah said. "They're taking care of Antoinette here. I haven't left her side since I came back. Do you remember what happened to you?"

"Yes. Every second. I have so much I need to tell you. I don't even know where to start." Her voice trailed off.

They embraced a second time.

"Do you remember anything? I mean, after you vanished?" Kris asked.

"Nothing. One moment I was in Sankofa Square with those crowds, then the next I was in Times Square with you."

Kris stared at her hands. The words felt too big, too strange. She almost swallowed them back. But then she lifted her eyes to meet her mother's.

"Mom...it was my proof. The Riemann hypothesis. That's what brought the orbs." She paused, her voice unsteady. "The aliens hid something inside it. A message. Math that's...way beyond us for now. Maybe I can help uncover more of it."

Sarah grabbed Kris's hand. She held it tight. "I never should have left you that morning. My job is to protect you both."

"It wasn't something you could change." Kris bowed her head. "The first time I went to the orbs, they said I wasn't ready," Kris said. "They were right. I wasn't ready to be myself."

Sarah looked past Kris as if she were looking out a window and into the past. Then she said, "I need you to listen to me. Listen and don't interrupt. People will think I'm crazy, but I have to tell you this.

"Before you were born, things with your father were bad. We fought all the time. One night after a terrible fight, I planned to take Antoinette and run. I cried myself to sleep. I dreamed of a girl with blond hair and green eyes, dressed in white, standing on a beach with waves behind her. There was something indescribable about her. And I knew it wasn't just a dream. I knew...I *knew* with every fiber of my being that I had to bring this girl into the world. That she was special. My purpose was to protect her.

"The next day I took a test. I was pregnant. After that, you and Antoinette were my whole world. You were the girl from my dream. My amazing girl. I love you and am so, so proud of you."

Sarah laughed through her tears. Kris glanced at Antoinette, watching her slow, rhythmic breathing.

"Einstein! For real, is that you?" Yolanda shouted from the doorway. She held Cindi, who barked and ran to her. Kris scratched behind her ears, and the little white dog nudged into her hand.

Kris reached out her arms, and Yolanda embraced her. "For real," Kris whispered.

Yolanda cleared her throat. "I was sure it was over. Then the people came back. And so did you," she said.

"Yolanda's been here with me every day," Sarah said. "She told me what happened. And she gave me your message. You said you'd come back to me, whatever it took."

"I waited here because I knew you'd come back to Sarah. At least I hoped you would. And I brought you this," Yolanda said, pulling her diary out of her bag.

Kris hugged her tight once more. "Thank you. Now, there's something I have to do before it is too late."

She sat on the side of Antoinette's bed and bowed her head. There was an ache in her soul that was deep and dark, but a kernel of silver light shone through. There was understanding. There was hope. And above all, there was love.

"You're not ready to go," Kris whispered to her sister. The white braid flickered in the distance for a long second. She leaned over Antoinette. "If you can hear me, Ant, it's time to wake up."

The medbed beeped, then beeped again. Sarah and Yolanda gasped.

Antoinette opened her eyes and blinked, focusing first on the ceiling, then on her sister's face. The bed's AI noted the change with a quiet blue pulsing light.

"K?" Antoinette muttered. Kris's eyes filled with tears of joy.

As Sarah clung to Antoinette, Kris rose and slipped away, walking down the long, winding corridor, past the startled guards, and through the secured entrance. The other part of this wasn't finished yet. She knew exactly where to go.

No one stopped her as she left the building. She walked and walked until she could make out a stretch of sky through the trees.

Far above her, almost out of sight, Kris spotted the small black orb hovering in the sky. A negligible dot in the blue expanse.

The orb was unmoving. Silent. Waiting.

I'm home, Kris thought. *The choice finally made sense.*

The orb shimmered, then vanished.

Kris slipped her hands into her pockets and walked back along the path, eager to be with her family again. Behind her, the branches swayed in the warm breeze as if nothing at all had changed.

ACKNOWLEDGEMENTS

T*HE SKY TOOK US* followed a long and winding path to publication, unfolding over more than a decade. As a mathematician, writing a novel was never a natural extension of my work, but this was a story I had to tell. It is a story about a young mathematical genius, first contact with a sophisticated alien species, the complexities of family, and the pull of ideas so powerful they threaten to carry us away. It's also about the quieter, tougher choices we face as we navigate our interior and exterior lives. Kris's journey through the book reflects all our journeys: our yearning for love, acceptance of our limitations, and transcendence.

I'm grateful to have worked with talented editors over the years, but I'd like to single out the inimitable author Kate Heartfield, without whom this book would not exist. My thanks as well to J Caleb Design for a striking cover that brings the book to life. I also want to thank Phillip Gessert for a terrific interior design.

My husband, Doug, deserves more gratitude than words allow, for his careful reading, wise counsel, and impeccable vegan lasagna. I am equally grateful to my sister Lisa and my mother, Anna Maria, for their steady support and willingness to engage with early versions of this story. Finally, I thank Aublis Press for shepherding this book from idea to finished page.

And to you, dear reader, thank you for choosing to spend a small fraction of your finite time with me, with Kris, and with the orbs.

Anthony Bonato is a mathematician and professor at Toronto Metropolitan University. He is the author of several books on graph theory and network science, as well as the popular mathematics book *Dots and Lines: Hidden Networks in Social Media, AI, and Nature*. His research explores how complex networks arise in mathematics, technology, and the natural world.

The Sky Took Us is his first novel. He lives in Toronto with his husband Doug.

www.ingramcontent.com/pod-product-compliance
Lightning Source LLC
Chambersburg PA
CBHW032018050726
47590CB00006B/2228